The Builder

Samer Bo

1

I was never a social person, always felt awkward around people and very shy to speak to anyone I don't know. At age 7, I showed extreme levels of intelligence. I was correcting my teachers daily even when they tried to give me complicated questions for much older students. There were no special programs for high intelligent kids in my small town so I was just moved to a higher grade, but later in the year I was still far ahead from my colleagues and was jumped again to a higher grade.

After 3 years, and at the age of 10 I was studying with the 15-year-old kids. I was still smarter than all of them, I didn't care about anything out of school, except reading. I spent my extra time in the library studying mathematics and physics. By the age of 12, I finished school and applied to university. I made the national news being the youngest boy to go to university and got a scholarship from the best university in the country.

I did a double major in physics and mathematics studies which took me 4 years to finish. I got my bachelor degree at age 16, then I started my masters in physics in the same university which took me another 2 years. At age of 18, I was applying for a PhD in the United States and United Kingdom. I received multiple scholarships from big universities but I have always been fascinated by London, so I chose one of the best universities in London.

The only thing I was interested in outside of school was sex. I found out I was gay at the age of 12, but being in Muslim country made it hard to explore. However, by the age of 16, and being surrounded by older guys, I was still able to hook up with a couple of guys who were on campus.

I arrived in London at the beginning of summer so I can have time to explore the city before starting the school year. It was about this time that I started to turn into a slut. My confidence in my looks had increased. In my teens, I had been slim and gangly. Now that I was 18, I was leaner and subtly toned. I kept my cute boyish looks with deep blue eyes and shaggy brown hair.

At the beginning of summer, I met a sexy, well hung 20-year-old bi, black lad called Leroy outside a gay bar. However, he was just into having me suck him off or fucking me. Being a pussy boy to one guy, suited me fine but didn't satisfy me totally so I started toilet trading. Toilet trading, also known as cottaging, is where you hang around public toilets (cottages) looking to meet other gay men. Most of the time I just used the glory hole and sucked any member that looked sexy and clean. Nine times out of ten I never knew the face of its owner. I didn't care either. All I knew was the pleasure of sucking on a hot hard cock and getting a gobful of hot thick tasty cum at the end.

My favourite cottage was in between college and home. It was also next to a building site where new houses where going up. As it was off the beaten path, it was mainly used by gays as a cottage.

There were 3 cubicles where, unlike modern toilets, had floor to ceiling dividing walls and doors. The two internal dividing walls had glory holes drilled out of them. The end wall had a peephole that looked out along the urinal trough. Then opposite the cubicles and urinal trough was a row of wash basins and hand dryers. There was gay graffiti all over the place and it could get quite busy.

It was the first week of the school year, I met my fellow PHD students and the professor that I will be working with. On my way home, I went to the toilets and took the centre cubical. No one was there so I read the gay graffiti on the walls and had a slow wank. After about 10 minutes, I heard someone come in and they went into the cubical on my right. I looked through the hole in the wall and found my eye was level with the crotch of a pair of jeans. They were dusty so I presumed he was one of the builders from the site over the road. I watched as he unzipped them and pushed them down, exposing his tight white briefs. I could see the outline of his big balls and semi-hard cock that was pointing up and to the left. I ran my finger round the edge of the glory hole to signal that I was the sucker. Then he pushed down his briefs and lifted the bottom of his light grey tee shirt.

What a sight it was, he had a toned, firm 6-pack stomach that was covered in light brown hairs leading down into a bush of light brown pubes. He had big low hanging balls that were lightly covered in soft brown pubes. His cock was semi-hard, uncut, and manly. Like his stomach, his cock and groin were also tanned but not to the extent his stomach was. He gave it a few wanks with his right hand to stir it into life. Once it was hard he pushed it and his balls through the glory hole.

With his erect tool and balls now on my side I could admire them properly. His cock was lightly tanned and about 7 inches long. It was a nice thickness, uncut, lightly veined, manly and very suckable. He had nice big low hanging balls that were lightly tanned, like his cock, with a few short brown pubes. I hoped they were full of man spunk for my cum hungry mouth.

After admiring his manly cock and balls I started lapping away at his sweaty balls. I swarmed my hot wet tongue all over them or lick a ball into my mouth and suck on it. I kept this up for a couple of minutes watching his manly cock throb above my face as I did so. I saw that his cock was oozing pre-cum, which had started trickling down the underside of his thick shaft. I stopped licking his balls and instead dragged my tongue up the underside of his hot hard throbbing cock, licking off the tasty pre-cum. I licked up to just under his swollen mushroom knob. When he was hard his foreskin pulled all the way back, exposing his swollen knob that was bigger than his shaft.

I licked up and down the underside of his throbbing manly cock a few times. Then I'd lick up the right side and then the left, either way I always stopped just short of his knob. I teased him like this for a bit until the urge to suck him off overcame me. I dragged my hot wet tongue over his balls, up the underside of his cock and over the underside of his knob. I started flicking my tongue over the sensitive area where he foreskin joined his knob; this caused him to drool even more tasty pre-cum onto my tongue.

After licking away at the underside of his knob for a bit I started swarming my tongue all over it, licking it like it was my favourite lollipop. I savoured the saltiness of his pre-cum and the spongy feeling of his knob on my tongue. As I licked his knob I felt his cock throb harder. I gave his swollen bulbous knob good licking before I took it into my mouth. I tightly clamped my lips around his throbbing shaft just below his knob. With his knob in my mouth I started to strongly suck on it as I continued to caress it with my tongue.

I spent a few minutes working on just his swollen sensitive knob. After that I relaxed my throat and started pushing my mouth down onto his cock. I slid my tightly clamped lips down his thick throbbing manly shaft taking in more and more. As I did so my tongue caressed the underside of his cock. I slid my hot wet mouth all the way down to the base of his cock, my nose buried in his pubes. I drank in his sweaty aroused manly aroma as his hot hard 7-inch meat throbbing in my cock hungry mouth, his large swollen knob plugging the back of my throat.

I started to deep throat his cock. I bobbed my mouth up and down the full length of his throbbing manly cock. As I sucked up and down, I wanked it with my lips and caressed it with my tongue, which I'd also swarm all over his sensitive knob when I reached the top. Having my ass fucked is my favourite sexual activity but sucking cock comes a very close second and I was certainly enjoying sucking on this cock. I had absolutely no idea what the guy looked like. All I knew was that he had a tanned toned stomach and hot sexy suckable cock.

I savoured having his manly penis in my mouth. I felt its warm throbbing pulse and silky hardness. I tasted the saltiness of his pre-cum and drank in his sweaty man aroused smell. I wanked it with my lips and caressed it with my tongue.

I sucked on his manly cock for ages although I was now only taking two thirds of it into my mouth as I was spending a bit more time working on his swollen sensitive knob. It was when my lips were close to the base of his cock that I felt a pulse travel through it and then felt a jet of hot cum blast down my throat. I quickly pulled my mouth up his cock and started flicking my tongue on the underside of his dick. I was just in time to catch the second blast on my tongue and it was a big one. Seven more big jets of cum rapidly followed that. I felt him filling my mouth with his strong hot thick salty man cum. I couldn't believe how much man spunk he was firing into my mouth.

When he shot the last of his load into my mouth, he pulled his spent cock out of my mouth and back through the glory hole. I still had his delicious man cum in my mouth, which I savoured before greedily swallowing it. I heard him leave so I realised that I wasn't going to have the favour returned. I was horny as fuck from the pleasure of sucking him off. My 6.5" 18-year-old cock was throbbing like mad. On top of that I now had the taste for sucking cock and drinking cum so I decided to hang about and see if anyone else came in.

After about ten minutes, I got bored as no one else came in so I decided to leave. But first, I had to take care of my own boner. I had been wearing surfer shorts with no underwear so I needed to cure my erection before I could pull them up. I couldn't walk through town with a boner tenting out the front of my shorts. The only way a boy can cure an erection is to toss it off. I stood up and firmly gripped it in my left hand. I started rapidly wanking it off as I recalled the cock sucking I had just performed. As I was hyper horny from sucking off the guy and now reliving it I didn't take me long to cum.

After tasting the strangers cum I was eager for more so when I felt the warning tingle in my cock I placed my cupped right hand in front of my cock. A couple more wanks with my left hand was all it took to have me spunking up into the cupped palm of my right hand. I loudly moaned as waves of sexual pleasure coursed through my body, radiating out from my cock, which was pumping jet after jet of hot cum into the palm of my hand.

When I shot the last of my load into my hand I brought it up to my face where I stuck my tongue in the pool of warm salty cum. I then tilted my head back and let my tasty cum flow out of my hand, over my tongue and down my throat. I then licked my palm clean as my hard on faded. I then pulled up my shorts and left.

2.

The following day after college, I was feeling horny so decided to use the cottage again. No one was there so I took the centre cubical as usual. I pulled down my shorts and sat on the toilet. No sooner had I got settled than someone took the cubical to my right. I looked through the hole and saw the crotch of some blue jeans and the bottom of a red tee shirt. They were both dusty so I wondered if it was the same guy I had sucked off the day before. I'd vaguely seen a guy wearing cut off jean shorts and a red sleeveless tee shirt, sat on a pile of bricks across the road, when I'd entered the toilet.

I watched as the guy unzipped his jeans and pushed them and his briefs down in one go. He was already hard and erect with his throbbing cock jutting straight out from his dense patch of brown pubes. It sure looked like the penis I had sucked off the previous day and this was confirmed when he lifted up the bottom of his red tee shirt, exposing his tanned hairy 6-pack stomach. I ran my finger around the edge of the glory hole to let him know I was ready. He thrust his throbbing erect manly cock and big balls through the glory hole. I admired them before gripping his throbbing cock and gave it a few wanks.

I then swarmed my tongue all over his swollen sensitive knob lapping up his tasty pre-cum and coating his knob in my saliva. I then kissed the tip before I push my lips down over his knob. They pasted over the thick ridge of his knob before tightly clamping around his thick throbbing shaft. I continued forcing my mouth onto his cock, taking more and more in until I had my nose buried in his sweaty pubes with all 7 inches of his manly cock throbbing in my mouth. I then started deep throating his hot sexy cock. As I sucked up and down it's throbbing length I wanked it with my lips and caressed it with my tongue.

I deep throated him for a couple of minutes before he pulled his cock out of my mouth and back through the glory hole.

"Did you suck me off yesterday?" He asked through the hole.

"Yes." I replied slightly disappointed at the stop of play.

"Want to come here and finish me off?" He asked.

First, I wasn't sure. If I went in and found I didn't fancy him I would find it hard to finish sucking him off. That is the wonder of glory holes all you must concentrate on is if the cock is sexy. Now I may be a cock sucking slut when it comes to using glory holes but when it comes to face to face encounters I can only do sex stuff with guys I like the look off. It would be awkward if I went in there and, then found he had the face like the back end of a bus. However, I was 18 and hormonally charged so they won out.

I pulled up my shorts and left my cubical and knocked on the door of his. He opened it up and I got my first view of him. And the view was a good one. I stepped into the cubical and locked the door behind me. I then turned to him to check him out. He had light brown hair and a handsome face, not dropped dead gorgeous or anything but still pleasing on the eye and looked to be in his late 20's. He had hazel eyes and a slender Roman nose. He had nice lush kissable lips. Then I took in the sight of his arms, which were very muscular and deeply tanned. It was obvious he worked out at the gym as well as his manual building work. He had bulging biceps and triceps with sinewy forearms that were covered in brown hairs. His tee shirt had a low-cut neck line so I could see his chest was covered in soft brown hairs. Then I looked at his sexy tanned throbbing manly cock, big balls, and his very muscular sexy tanned hairy legs. All in all, he was a fit sexy hunk of a man and certainly had my motor running.

Whereas I had been worried that he may have been ugly I was now worried that as he'd seen me he wouldn't be interested. I was worried that he would back now that he had seen I am not as good looking as he likes. However, he didn't object and instead moved to the side to give me access to the toilet. I sat on the toilet and he stood in front of me.

"What's your name?" He asked his cock throbbing in my face. I managed to tear my gaze from it and look up at his face as I told him my name.

"I'm Arnold." He replied.

"You have a sexy cock." I said as I took it in my left hand and gave it a few wanks, feeling its warm throbbing hardness.

"Thanks, and you are a great cock sucker. You get much action here?"

"I've sucked a few. Not been coming here that long." I replied still mesmerised by his manly cock.

"From the way you sucked me off yesterday, I thought you were older. I'm surprised you can suck cock like that at your age."

"Thanks." I said swelling with pride.

"How old are you?"

"21." I lied fearing that he would back out if he found out my true age. Arnold was unconvinced.

"Doesn't bother me kid, I ain't going to back out. You got me too horny for that and it's obvious you're no stranger to this."

"OK I'm 18." I replied.

"Well for an 18-year-old, you suck dick like a pro." He said as he slapped his swollen knob on my lips.

"I'm 27. You OK with that?" He added

I replied by opening my lips and taking his knob into my mouth and tightly clamping my lips around his throbbing shaft just below the ridge of his knob. I started sucking and licking away on his sensitive knob which was drooling tasty pre-cum onto my tongue. As I sucked on his knob I swarmed my hands all over his fit body. I caressed his muscular hairy thighs and reached round to grope his firm toned ass that was covered in soft downy hairs. I'd also stick my hands up his tee shirt where I stroked his rippled lightly haired stomach and grope his toned hairy pecs. I mainly prefer smooth guys but I appreciate that some body hair can be sexy too and Arnold had the right amount to make him look sexy and manly without being a turn off.

After giving his knob a good working over I relaxed my throat and slid my hot wet mouth all the way down onto his manly cock, taking in all throbbing inches and burying my nose in his pubes.

"Fuck yeah!" Arnold moaned as he had his 27-year-old cock engulfed in the mouth of an 18-year-old lad. I then started deep throating his cock, sliding my hot wet sucking mouth up and down it, wanking it with my lips and caressing it with my tongue. I savoured the taste of his salty pre-cum and the sponginess of his hard cock on my tongue. Then there was the warm throbbing hardness of his chopper in my mouth and the feel its veins under my caressing tongue. I also drank in his strong musky sweaty manly-aroused aroma.

I deep throated his cock for a good few minutes and from the way Arnold was moaning he certainly seemed to be enjoying it.

"Kid, do you take it up the ass too?" Arnold asked as I sucked on his cock. I reluctantly took my mouth off his hot manly cock to answer.

"Defo. It's my fave." I said before I took just his swollen knob into my mouth where I started sucking on it and swarming my tongue all over it.

"Do you want that cock up your ass?" He asked.

"You want to?" I asked surprised that a hunk like him would want to fuck a boy like me.

"Fuck yeah, you're well cute."

"I def want to be fucked by a hunk like you." I said. I then rummaged in my bag and pulled out a tube of KY jelly.

As I started lubing up his hot hard throbbing groin, Arnold gripped the bottom of his red tee shirt and lifted it up and hooked it over his head, but with his arms still in it. My eyes bulged at the gorgeous sight before me. I took in the sight of his tanned, washboard, lightly haired stomach, and his very toned pecs, which were dusted in brown hairs. He really had a fit, toned sexy hunky body that was practically making me drool.

With his cock lubed up I stood up and pushed down my shorts, the front of which were soaked in my pre-cum. I turned around and bent over, using my hands to steady myself on the cistern of the toilet. I felt Arnold start rubbing his hot hard cock up and down my ass crack searching out my hole. He soon found it and increased the pressure. My ass ring briefly resisted before finally giving way. When his swollen knob popped open my ass ring I let out a moan of pleasure. It became a protracted moan of pleasure as Arnold slowly forced his hot hard throbbing cock ball deep into my ass. I felt his pubed groin pressed up against my smooth ass with all 7 throbbing inches of his thick manly cock throbbing in my teen boy ass. I savoured feeling his hot hard cock throbbing in my ass and he enjoyed having my tight teen ass wrapped around his cock.

"Fuck me hard." I lustily begged, looking over my right shoulder at the hunky guy who had his cock up my ass.

With my go ahead, Arnold started fucking me with long, deep, hard powerful thrusts using all of his cock. He pulled his cock all the way out of my ass. I felt my ass and pucker sucking on his retreating cock. His manhood popped open my sphincter as he pulled out. There was a brief pause before he slammed back in again. His swollen cock popped open my ass ring. I then felt it force open the walls of my ass as he rammed his hot hard cock deep into my ass.

"Fuck yeah!" I moaned as I had my pussy boy ass impaled on his manly cock.

For a good couple of minutes, Arnold used the full length of his cock on my ass, pulling all the way out before slamming back in ball deep. His large swollen knob gave my ass ring a dam good working over as he slammed his cock in and out of my ass. I then felt his knob caress the walls of my sensitive ass, as his shaft stimulated my ass lips. He was really giving me a good fuck, using all his muscular strength to pound my pussy boy ass. My ass ring became swollen and tender at the rough hard fucking it was getting but there was no real pain but loads of pleasure.

After a couple of minutes, Arnold stopped pulling his cock out of my ass. Instead he would pull back until the ridge of his swollen knob hit the inside of my ass ring then he would slam it all back in. As I had a hunky man pounding my tight teen boy ass, I firmly gripped my cock in my left hand and started wanking it off as vigorously as he was fucking my ass.

"Fuck yeah, you're doing me good." I moaned as I felt his hot, hard, thick, throbbing, meaty cock pounding my hot, wet, tight, sensitive ass. Waves of pleasure radiated from my ass but I would get the odd stab of pain, which reminded just how hard he was fucking my ass. Arnold was moaning with pleasure as he valued the sensations of ploughing the steamy tight ass of a boy almost 10 years younger.

We were both lost in the intensity of stranger on stranger sleazy sex. I hardly knew the guy but being a horny teen slut, I was happy to bend over for him. I may have been an easy lay, just as happy with shags as I was with relationships, but the guy had to be sexy to get into my ass. Then we heard the door to the toilets open. Arnold reacted quickly and slammed all 7 throbbing inches of his man cock into my teen ass. Then he pushed us both forwards. We heard someone go into the cubical next to us. If the new arrival looked in through the glory hole all he would see was Arnold's ass so it would look like he was stood taking a piss.

Arnold and I waited with bated breath for the guy to either do his business and leave or signal he was gay and cottaging too. It didn't take long before the new guy circled the glory hole. Arnold and I had the green light. With Arnold's hands on my hips and his cock buried up my ass Arnold moved us both backwards. He then started pounding my ass again. He fucked me as fast and furiously as he had before but now we knew we had an audience on the other side of the dividing wall. This turned me on even more. Here I was an 18-year-old lad bent over and wanking in a public toilet with a complete stranger powerfully fucking my ass as another stranger watched. The sleazy location, the fact that we were watched and the sensations of being fucked so hard by such a hunky man all made me hyper horny.

Arnold carried on fucking me bent over for a few minutes. Then he gripped my shoulders and pulled me up so that I was stood upright. He then twisted us both around and pushed me up against the wall. The guy on the other side had been circling his finger around the glory hole signalling he wanted to suck. My raging hard teen cock and balls went through the glory hole. Arnold pressed me right up against the dividing wall and I twisted my head to the left so that my right cheek was pressed up against the wall. Out of the corner of my left eye I saw the look of lust on the handsome face of the hunky stranger who was fucking me like a slut. Arnold interlocked the fingers of each of his hands with mine before lifting them above my head.

Arnold then began pounding my tender tight teen ass with renewed vigour. I felt his sweaty pubed groin rapidly and rhythmically slapping against my pert smooth ass. His hot thick throbbing veiny shaft was stretching and stimulating my tender ass ring, his pubes tickling it. His swollen knob forced open and caressed the walls of my love tunnel, hitting my prostate. I was delirious with the pleasure of being passionately and powerfully fucked by a stocky stranger, my well-fucked, tight, teen ass sucking away at his pounding manly cock. Arnold was really satisfying my pussy boy needs.

On top of the wonderful feeling of being fucked really rough and hard by a hot guy, the guy on the other side opened his mouth and took half my cock into his mouth. I moaned louder with pleasure as I felt the guy on the other side of the glory hole wrap his lips half way down my 6.5" member. With half my cock in his mouth he began greedily sucking up and down it. He worked his hot wet sucking mouth up and down my cock, wanking it with his lips and caressing it with my tongue.

I purred with pleasure as a stranger, who I had no idea of what he looked like, worked his hot wet sucking mouth up and down my teen cock as a hunky guy whose face I could see, pounded my ass. I felt so horny and slutty. There was the smell of the public toilet mixing with man and teen sweat, hormones and gay sex.

"You're such a hot fuck." Arnold moaned in my ear as his manly cock sank ball deep into my teen ass again. I just moaned with pleasure lost in the intensity of the situation.

It all rapidly got too much. "I'm going to cum." I gasped. Seconds later I was loudly moaning and groaning with pleasure as I had an intense orgasm into the hot wet mouth of a guy I had no idea of what he looked like. All the stimulations had led to me having a big powerful orgasm.

As I orgasmed my tight ass began to spasm uncontrollably around Arnold's hard thrusting manly cock. I felt him pick up his fucking pace, pounding my ass even harder and faster than ever. Orgasming made my ass even more sensitive so it was really feeling the good hard fucking Arnold was giving it. It felt very tender and abused but also very pleasurable and satisfied. I was just swept along with it all.

"Oh yeah, give it to me!" I begged Arnold in total slutty pussy boy mode. My favourite sex is when a guy really uses me hard to please himself.

As my orgasm died down Arnold launched into an intense fucking frenzy. I was moaning at the pounding my tight tender ass was getting. His hot hard thick manly cock was pounding my ass so hard I thought he would start a fire, he'd sure set my ass on fire with pleasure. My buttocks were mildly stinging from the slapping of his sweaty pubed groin banging against them. The walls of my ass were glowing with the pleasure of being rapidly rubbed and stimulated by his swollen knob.

"Want my cum?" Arnold moaned as he continued his frantic fucking of my ass.

"Fuck yeah. Fill me with your man spunk." I begged, eagerly to feel this sexy hunky guy cumming in my ass. Arnold gave me a few more long, deep, hard powerful thrust before he rammed his cock home. His sweaty pubed groin loudly slapped against my buttocks as he drove his hot hard thick throbbing manly cock ball deep into my hot, wet, tight, quivering, well-fucked, teen pussy boy ass.

"Fuck yeah!" Arnold growled as I felt his manly cock swell, throb, and pulse in my ass as it powerfully blasts jet after jet of hot man cum deep into my tender ass. I just purred with pleasure as I felt this sexy hunky stranger fill my teen boy ass with his hot man cum.

As Arnold had a big and powerful orgasm in my ass the other guy was still sucking on my spent cock. This was getting slightly uncomfortable as my penis was now suffering from post orgasm hyper sensitivity but I couldn't back away as Arnold had me impaled on his orgasming cock pressed up against the wall so I couldn't back off. Once Arnold's orgasm had died down he kept his spent cock in my tender, well-fucked cummy ass. Luckily the guy on the other side of the glory hole had given up on my cock which had now gone soft.

Arnold's cock slowly went soft and then plopped out of my ass.

"I think we both needed that." Arnold whispered.

"Defo." I said still glowing from the awesome fucking. I watched as Arnold adjusted his tee shirt, covering up his tanned, toned, hairy upper body. Then I watched him pull up his cut of jean shorts and boxers. I then pulled up my shorts.

We both left together but once we were outside he walked off in the opposite direction without saying a word. Part of me wondered if I should catch him up and tell him I would like this to become regular. But the self-doubt kicked and I just thought he wouldn't be interested in me. I'd just been lucky that I'd caught him when he was real horny and now that he had dumped his load in my ass he'd have no further use for me.

On the walk to the bus station and the ride hole I felt his cum leaking out of my satisfied ass that still had the dull throbbing pleasure you only get after a good rough hard fucking. That night in bed I had a good long slow wank thinking about the fucking I had received that afternoon.

3.

The following day, after college, I practically ran to the public toilets. When I got there, it was empty so I took up my usual centre cubicle. I was in there for 30 minutes and only two guys came in and they used the urinal for what it was meant for and quickly left. I had guessed that now Arnold had had his fun with a teen he wasn't interested.

On Friday I went back to the toilets. I wasn't expecting to see Arnold ever again but was hoping for at least some cock sucking action. However, when I got there I saw Arnold sat on the pile of bricks by the building site. He signalled me over. As I walked over to him I saw he was wearing a tight white muscles top and his cut off jean shorts.

"Hi" I said as I watched at his handsome face and his well muscular hunky arms and legs.

"Were you going in there for some action?" He asked.

"Yes." I said feeling a little embarrassed at what this hunky man might think of my toilet trading.

"You looking for another fucking?"

"if you are offering?" I said as I smiled at him. He smiled back and said

"So, you liked it?"

"It was fucking ace." I honestly replied.

"Bet a cutie like you has bent over for loads of guys in there."

"Not at all! you were the first fuck from there, honestly. I'll suck anyone off if I can't see them and their cock looks sexy and clean, but I only let sexy guys fuck me."

"But I am sure you have been fucked a few times."

"No. I lost my cherry at 14 to a friend and had quite a few guys since then. Mainly teens but did had a one time with an older man"

"Well you were a great fuck, sure know how to take cock."

"Thanks." I said swelling with pride. Our chat had also got me hard and as I was going commando, my hard cock was tenting out the front of my shorts.

"I want to fuck you now." Arnold said as he grabbed the front of his jeans.

"Sweet. Do you have a place?" Was my reply.

"Follow me we can use one of the new houses. Will be safer than the bogs." Arnold said as he jumped off the pile of bricks.

As he led the way we chatted to find out more about each other. It was now that I found out his surname was Savage and that he was a plasterer. We went into one of the houses that was almost finished and went upstairs into one of the bedrooms. The only thing in the room was a table.

"Come and give me a kiss" Arnold said.

I turned to face him and looked up at his face. I was 5' 9" to his 6' 1".

Arnold then started to passionately kiss me, which I returned.

As we passionately kissed, I stuck my hand up his tee shirt and started caressing his toned hairy pecs and stomach. After a bit, I lifted his tee shirt. I exposed his tanned, toned, fit washboard stomach that was lightly covered in soft brown hairs. Then I exposed his very toned, nicely defined, tanned pecs which were covered in soft brown hairs. As his tee shirt came off over his head I exposed his sweaty lickable armpits which had small tufts of sweat matted brown hairs. I admired his handsome tanned face and hazel eyes. I also observed his tanned muscular toned arms and well-toned upper body. I found his sweaty manly aroma intoxicating.

I briefly kissed him before I lifted his left arm, exposing his sweaty armpit. I dove in and began eagerly licking away at his pit. I drank in its musky sweaty smell and savoured the salty taste of his sweat and felt its hairs tickle my tongue. The smell and taste really turned me on; my rock-hard cock was soaking the front of my shorts in pre-cum

"Mmm yeah lick my sweaty pit." Arnold moaned.

I gave his left sweaty pit a good licking out before Arnold raised his right arm and said

"Now do my right pit."

I eagerly obeyed and began licking it out, savouring the taste and smell. This hunk was really turning me on. I could see and sense he had the muscles, age and experience to treat me like the slutty pussy boy I was.

Once I'd licked his right pit out I licked over his right pec to his nipple. I began circling my tongue around and then over his small light brown nipple. As I did this I rubbed my fingers over his left nipple. I felt both his nipples hard and once they were I began to gently chew on his right nip as I pinched his left nips.

"Fuck yeah, abuse my nips." Arnold moaned. Like me Arnold liked having his nipples roughly played with so I started chewing and pinching them harder. I kept swapping between them. If I chew one I pinched the other and then swapped over.

I did that until both his light brown nipples were red and swollen. I then started kissing and licking down the centre ridge of his firm, hairy, washboard stomach to the waistband of his jeans. I stroked the outline of his hard cock before I undid his jeans and pulled them down his tanned, muscular hairy legs along with his briefs.

I exposed his dense sweaty patch of brown pubes and then the base of his thick throbbing manly rod. As I pulled down his jeans and briefs down, more of his cock came into view. When the waistband pasted his knob, his cock sprang back and slapped his stomach. Then I saw his big low hanging balls before exposing his very sexy muscular thighs and then lower legs. I admired the sight of his sexy manly cock before me. I then tightly gripped it in my left hand and peeled back his foreskin.

With his knob exposed, I started swarming my hot wet tongue all over it, causing Arnold to purr with pleasure. I savoured the taste of his pre-cum and the sponginess of his knob. Then without warning I relaxed my throat and in one go thrust my hot wet mouth all the way down onto his manly cock. I buried my nose in his sweaty pubes and tightly clamped my lips around the base of his 7" cock.

"Fuck yeah, eat my cock." Arnold gasped as he had a cock hungry boy take all of his man cock into his mouth. I felt all 7 inches of his cock throbbing in my mouth as I drank in the heady musky sweaty aroused aroma of his groin.

I continued deep throating his thick throbbing manly cock. I slid my sucking mouth on his hot hard cock, wanking it with my lips and caressing it with my tongue. I dragged my tightly clamped lips up from the pubed base of his cock, up along the throbbing, veiny shaft and up to the swollen knob, which I sucked and licked.

"That's so fucking good." Arnold gasped as I sucked away on his manhood. I was so fucking horny from sucking off this sexy hunky guy. My teen cock was wildly throbbing and drooling pre-cum into my shorts, causing a big obvious damp patch to form on the front. As I sucked away on his cock, Arnold pulled my tee shirt off over my head.

I greedily sucked away on his hot cock for a while before Arnold said

"I want to fuck your hot ass."

He hooked his hands under my arms and lifted me up. We passionately kissed as Arnold pushed down my shorts releasing my rampant teen cock.

"Get on your back on the table." Arnold instructed.

I obeyed and lay on my back and gripped my legs behind my knees and pulled them back, exposing my ass. I watched Arnold spit on his manly cock.

Arnold stood before me and I felt him rub his swollen knob up and down my ass crack, searching out my hole. I felt him press his knob against my sphincter. I took time to admire his handsome face and tanned, muscular, hunky body, however we were both as eager as each other to have his hot hard manly cock up my tight ass.

The pressure of his knob increased on my ass ring, which briefly resisted before giving way. I gasped with pleasure as his cock popped open my pucker and in one deep hard powerful thrust he rammed all 7 throbbing inches of his manly cock ball deep into my ass.

"Fuck yeah." I gasped in pleasure at having my pussy boy ass powerfully penetrated.

"So hot and tight." Arnold moaned in pleasure as he had my steamy hot wet tight teen ass wrapped around his cock. Arnold held his cock ball deep in me for a while so we could both enjoy the sensation and I felt his thick manly cock throbbing in my ass.

Arnold started fucking me with long deep hard powerful thrusts of his hot cock. He would pull back his cock until the ridge of his knob hit the inside of my ass ring, my ass and pucker sucking at his retreating cock. He'd then powerfully rammed it back in ball deep, his swollen knob forcing open and caressing the walls of my ass and hitting my prostate. My ass lips wanked his thick throbbing shaft, which stimulated them.

"Yeah, fuck me hard" I begged.

"You love it hard up the ass, don't you?"

"I am a cock loving pussy boy." I gasped as I felt his penis hit my prostate again.

As Arnold fucked me hard, I watched his tanned, hairy washboard stomach ripple, looked up at his toned hairy pecs and handsome face. Each rough hard powerful thrust sent waves of pleasure through me. He was really pounding my tight teen ass and I was loving it. Arnold lent forward and started kissing me. I returned the kiss and started groping his sweaty, hairy toned pecs and pinched his nipples. My ass was on fire with the pleasure of being fucked fast and hard by the hot thick cock of this guy. As he fucked me I drank in his sweaty manly-aroused aroma.

"Fucking do me harder!" I begged, totally swept up in slutty lust for this hunky man. I needed him to fuck me senseless and feel my ass throbbing from a good hard fucking. Arnold responded by standing up. He was now stood upright with me laid on the table at a 90-degree angle to him. I had a tight grip on the edge of the table to stop my body being pushed away from him when he rammed his hot hard manly cock forward. Also, being stood up meant that Arnold could get maximum penetration and as it went in at an upward angle his swollen knob hit my prostate on every thrust. Arnold had a tight grip on my hips and was using them to pull himself into my well-fucked ass.

The room was full of the heady aroma of sex, sweat and hormones. There were our uninhibited moans and groans of sexual pleasure, the squelch of my ass sucking on his pounding cock and the loud rhythmic slapping of his groin against my ass. Our bodies were glistening in sweat and we were both flushed with the exertion of rough passionate sex.

I admired the looks of pleasure and exertions as they played across his handsome face. I extended my arm to touch his tanned toned hairy pecs then I roughly pinched his hard-erect nipples. I watched his hairy washboard stomach ripple as I felt his hot hard cock pounding my cock hungry ass. All of it had me seriously turned on and I could feel myself racing towards orgasm even though my cock wasn't being touched.

Any 18-year old boy is always horny but on top of that here I was laid on a decorating table, on a building site, as a hunky 27-year old builder fucked my young, precocious, cock hungry, teen boy ass senseless. Each hard, powerful thrust of his thick manly cock set my ass on fire with pleasure and hit my G spot, causing my raging teen hard on to wildly throb and drool pre-cum onto my stomach. I knew I couldn't hold out much longer.

I relished the pleasure of being fucked hard for as long as I could while fighting my own orgasm but it was all too much.

"I'm going to cum!" I yelled as I felt the warm warning tingle rapidly melt into the hot raging torrent of cum racing up my throbbing cock and powerfully blasting out. The first two jets were so powerful they hit my face and instinctively my tongue darted out of my mouth and licked my own cum from my face. These two were followed by five more jets, which splashed all over my smooth chest and stomach. I loudly moaned and groaned with intense sexual pleasure as orgasmic waves washed through my body.

"Fuck yeah." Arnold moaned as he saw me orgasm all over myself with my hot wet tight teen ass spasming around his pounding cock. The sight and sensation of having my orgasm on his cock pushed him over the edge. With one final deep, hard powerful thrust he rammed his hot, hard, thick, throbbing, meaty cock ball deep into my ass. The thrust was so hard I saw stars. I then felt his cock swell, throb, and pulse as it powerfully blasted jet after jet of hot man jiz deep into my ass.

We both moaned and groaned with pleasure as he filled my teen boy cunt with his man cum. I felt every throb and pulse of his cock in my ass as man and teen boy became fussed in the most intimate way. When his orgasm died down he collapsed on top of me. I felt his hot sweaty manly hairy chest and stomach press against my sweaty smooth teen body.

We stayed like that for a minute or two, both of us trying to get our breath back. As we did so I enjoyed feeling his sweaty, hunky, slightly hairy manly body pressed against my smooth body. I drank in his strong sweaty, manly, aroused aroma and felt his cock slowly grow soft in my ass.

"Fuck I hope you enjoyed this as I did, kid." Arnold moaned as he pulled his spent cock out of my tender well-fucked teen ass.

"Sure did." I moaned still in the post orgasm glow. I then stood up and we both began to passionately kiss.

After a couple of minutes kissing, I lifted up his left arm and exposed his sweaty armpit. I dove straight in and licked it out before doing the same with his right. We both moaned with pleasure as I did so and I savoured the smell and taste of his armpits.

4.

Just before Arnold & I parted on the Friday, he invited me around to his flat on Saturday afternoon. I eagerly agreed and he gave me directions.

The following day I put on a white tracksuit, with no underwear and a light blue tee shirt. It was a real struggle walking to Arnold's without popping a boner. I was so excited about having another hot sex session with hunky Arnold and also the satiny material of my trackies felt so dam good rubbing against my naked teen cock.

When I got to Arnold's flat I knocked on the door. I had to wait a bit before Arnold answered. When he did, I saw that he was just wearing a pair of white shorts and trainers. His sexy, toned, manly body was sweaty so it was obvious that he had been working out. I had time to admire his handsome face, which broke out in a sexy smile when he saw it was me. My gaze then took in the sight of his tanned, bulging arms and toned pecs. The patch of chest hairs was matted with sweat. My eyes then went down his tanned, firm, lightly haired washboard stomach. I was also able to get a good look at his tanned, muscular legs before Arnold invited me in.

I followed Arnold as he led me into the Living room. This was a large room with three small sofas and a large TV. In a corner he had created a work out area. There was an exercise bike and rowing machine as well as some free weights and an exercise mat. "You caught me doing my exercises. Mind if I finish them?" Arnold asked. "I will watch." I replied with a wink.

I took the sofa opposite the workout area. I sat slouched down and my legs automatically opened. Arnold started his exercises by bending down and picking up a dumbbell in each hand. He then started doing bicep curls. I watched his arm muscles, especially his biceps, flex as he lifted the weights up and down. His pecs also flexed as he lifted the weights.

Watching Arnold doing bicep curls, with his toned muscles flexing and bulging, started turning me on. It was definitely a very sexy sight. As I watched him work out I felt my cock begin to stir. In no time at all it was standing at its full 6.5 inches and straining against the satiny material of my white trackies bottoms, forming a tent in the front. Arnold spent about 20 minutes finishing off his exercise routine as I watched. By the time he finished exercising my teen cock was wildly throbbing in my trackies, which now had a large and obvious pre-cum damp patch on the front.

"Looks like someone is horny." Arnold said as his gaze went down to the tent in the front of my trackies. "I'm not the only one." I said as I noticed the outline of his thick manly cock down the left leg of his shorts. "Exercising always turns me on." Arnold said as he walked over to me and stood in front of me.

I sat upright so that my face was close to his covered cock. I looked up at his handsome face as I started rubbing his hard-erect cock through the material of his shorts and briefs. I then hooked my fingers under the waistband of his shorts and briefs and started pulling them down.

First, I exposed his dense patch of brown pubes and then the base of his thick manly cock. As I pulled his shorts down, more of his cock came into view. His cock sprang up and bounced about as I pulled his shorts all the way down his legs. Arnold was now stood before me totally naked except for his shorts around his ankles and the trainers on his feet.

I took in the sight of his sexy hunky body before me. I admired the sight of his sweaty hairy chest and firm washboard stomach. Then there was the sight of his dense patch of pubes above his thick, throbbing, veiny manly cock. His big balls hung low under his cock, covered in brown hairs. My gaze then went to his tanned, muscular hairy legs.

Seeing Arnold naked sure was an erotic sight and seeing his hard cock throbbing inches from my face had my mouth watering. I firmly gripped his cock in my hand and aimed it upwards, exposing his big sweaty balls. I started licking away at his nuts, tasting the saltiness of his sweat and drinking in his strong sweaty manly aroma. Arnold purred with pleasure as I lapped away at his balls.

I licked away at his balls for a while, occasionally taking one of them into my mouth and rolling it about. However, the urge to take his thick throbbing manly cock into my mouth soon became irresistible. I dragged my tongue from the base of his cock and up the sensitive underside. I felt the silkiness of his skin and the veiny throbbing pulse of his cock as I dragged my tongue closer to his swollen knob. I stopped just short of his knob before dragging my tongue back down his cock.

I repeated this several times, working my tongue up and down the underside of his cock but ignoring his knob. Then I licked up the left-hand side but also stopped short of his knob before going back down. I then went up the right-hand side. I then spent awhile alternating between licking the left, right or underside of his throbbing cock. By stopping short of his cock, I was teasing him and he was eager to get his cock in my mouth.

I teased him for a while longer before I kissed the tip of his cock, tasting the pearl of per-cum that was there. I then relaxed my mouth and started pushing my hot wet mouth down his cock. My moist lips parted and slid down over his swollen sensitive knob, over its thick ridge and tightly clamped them around his shaft, just below the ridge of his knob. I gave his knob a brief suck and lick before I forced the rest of my mouth onto his cock. I took all 7 throbbing inches into my mouth until my nose was buried in his dense patch of sweaty pubes, all of his manly cock throbbing in my mouth, with his knob pushing on the back of my throat.

I bobbed my hot, wet, sucking, cock hungry mouth up and down his thick throbbing meaty cock. I took it in all the way in to the pubed base before pulling back so that just his swollen knob was in my mouth. As I sucked on his cock I wanked it with my lips, caressed it with my tongue and greedily sucked away on it. My hands swarmed all over his very sexy muscular tanned hairy thighs and reached around to grope his toned ass.

"Oh yeah suck my cock." Arnold moaned as I worked my experienced mouth up and down his manhood. With each lunge of my mouth I felt his cock throbbing, tasted the saltiness of his pre-cum and drank in his strong sweaty musky aroused aroma. My own cock was wildly throbbing and drooling pre-cum into my trackies, making the damp patch on the front even bigger and more obvious.

I deep throated Arnold for a while before I pulled my mouth up and just concentrated on his swollen sensitive knob. I greedily sucked away at his knob and swarmed my tongue all over it, savouring his pre-cum. As I sucked on his knob, Arnold ran his fingers through my shaggy hair and moaned words of encouragement. I felt so fucking horny by the fact that even though I was only 18, I had the pleasure of sucking off a fit sexy hunky 27-year-old guy. I'm a bottom boy so was born to suck cock and take it up the ass so I was just fulfilling my function but loving every second of it.

I started alternating my sucking style as I felt Arnold's level of horniness increase. One minute I would be concentrating on just sucking his swollen sensitive knob and swarming my tongue all over it. The next I was deep throating his cock, wanking it with my tightly clamped lips and taking all 7 throbbing inches into my mouth right down to the pubed hilt. Or I was licking up and down the sides and underside of his cock or licking and sucking away at his balls.

All the time I was doing this my hands were caressing over his fit hunky body. My hands felt his firm toned hairy thighs before going around to grope his pert ass or they'd caress his firm lightly haired washboard stomach.

I sucked away on Arnold's cock for ages, varying my sucking style to keep him interested and to increase his horniness. I could sense that he was getting close to orgasm. His moans and groans of pleasure were becoming louder and more frequent. His cock was throbbing harder in my mouth and his breathing was becoming faster and more laboured. These were the signs for me to pick up my sucking pace.

I stopped alternating my style and instead concentrated on bobbing my wet sucking mouth up and down his cock. On most lunges I would take about two thirds of his throbbing manly cock into my mouth and on others I would take in all 7 inches and bury my nose in his sweaty pubes. When I did that his swollen knob would plug the back of my throat where I would flex my throat muscles on his knob before sucking my mouth back up his rod. As I sucked away on his manhood

I wanked it with my lips and caressed it with my tongue.

"Fuck kid I'm close." Arnold gasped so I pulled my mouth up to the tip of his cock where I strongly sucked away on his knob and swarmed my tongue all over it, paying particular attention to the very sensitive spot on the underside of his knob where his foreskin joined. I also started rubbing a finger of my right hand around his ass lips, causing him to moan with pleasure.

Arnold's breathing increased even further and his body started to shake slightly as the pressure of orgasm rapidly built up in him. I increased my efforts still further, overcoming the ache in my mouth to suck on his knob harder and faster and flick my tongue all over it.

Arnold managed to hold out for a bit longer as I concentrated on sucking and licking his knob. Then I felt his whole-body tense up just as he cried "I'm going to cum!" I then felt his cock swell in my mouth and felt the pulse race down it before his first jet of hot thick tasty man spunk blasted out of his cock and coated my tongue. Arnold loudly moaned and groaned with pleasure as an intense orgasm flowed through his body. I muffled a moan of pleasure as I felt my mouth filling with his hot tasty cum.

The first jet was followed by 6 more big powerful spurts of cum, filling my mouth with his man seed. I felt every pulse of his cock as he pumped his spunk into my cum hungry mouth and I held it there to savour its taste and texture. I then greedily gulped down his cum before I started gently sucking on his spent cock until it became too sensitive. "That was fucking ace. I sure needed to cum." Arnold breathlessly moaned. "You can cum in my mouth anytime." I replied. "Looks like you need to cum too." Arnold said, his gaze dropping to the tent and wet spot in my tracksuit bottoms. I just smiled back at him.

Arnold then dropped to his knees and hooked his fingers under the waistband of my trackies. He then started pulling them down and I lifted up my ass so that he could pull them down. He pulled them all the way down to my ankles, releasing my throbbing 6.5" uncut teen cock.

I watched his handsome face as he firmly gripped my cock in his right hand. A shiver of pleasure ran through my body as he engulfed my cock in the warm firm grip of his hand. He then gave my cock a few wanks before he pulled back my foreskin, exposing my swollen pinky red knob. I then watched as he opened his mouth and moved it over my cock and engulfed the head. He tightly clamped his moist lips around my throbbing shaft just below the ridge of my knob.

With the tip of my cock in his hot wet mouth he began to greedily suck away at it and swarm his tongue all over it. Waves of sexual pleasure coursed down my cock and through my body as I had a sexy hunky 27-year-old man expertly suck my teen cock. Not only were there the intense pleasurable feelings of his hot wet mouth sucking my sensitive cock but there was also the highly erotic sight of his handsome face impaled on the end of my young cock.

Arnold spent a couple of minutes just sucking and licking away on my swollen sensitive knob making me purr with pleasure and my cock throb wildly. As he did so he used his big strong hands to caress my lean toned lightly haired thighs. I moaned words of encouragement as Arnold worked his oral magic on my 18-year-old cock.

Arnold then started bobbing his hot wet strongly sucking mouth up and down my cock, wanking it with his tightly clamped lips and caressing the sensitive underside and knob with his tongue. This felt so dam good and had me moaning with pleasure and my cock wildly throbbing. I was already highly turned on from the pleasure of sucking him off and now that he was sucking me off I was getting even hornier.

Soon Arnold was deep throating me, taking in all 6.5" cock my cock right down to the pubed base. I felt the hot wetness of his sucking mouth engulfing my cock. His lips wanked my cock as he worked his mouth up and down, with his tongue caressing it. All the while I was watching his handsome face bobbing up and down my cock.

Arnold spent a blissful age sucking on my cock before I felt my cum starting to boil in my balls. I could feel the pressure building and knew I was close to orgasm. My breathing became faster and louder and I could feel my body tensing up. I moaned to Arnold that I was getting close and he pulled his mouth up my cock and concentrated on sucking and licking just my swollen sensitive knob.

Having him suck and lick my knob made me hyper horny and started the warning tingle in my balls. I desperately fought the urge to cum so that I could prolong the wonderful blow job Arnold was giving me. However, it was a lost cause. It only took a few more licks and sucks of my knob before the pleasure got too much.

My whole body tensed up as I felt the pressure in my balls reach critical mass. I felt my cock swell as the first bolt of cum race down it. "Oh, fuck yeah!" I loudly cried out as the first jet of cum exploded out of my cock, sending waves of intense pleasure through me. Arnold heightened the pleasure by continuing to suck on my knob and flick the tip of his tongue on the underside of my knob where my foreskin joined.

My first jet was quickly followed by another. I loudly moaned and groaned with pleasure as I pumped more cum into his mouth. I felt Arnold holding my cum in his mouth, my cock becoming surrounded by my cum and Arnold's hot wet mouth.

I had a big intense orgasm, pumping several big jets of cum into Arnold's mouth. He kept his mouth on the end of my cock as I orgasmed, my cum filling his mouth as he gently sucked on my knob. When my orgasm finished, he pulled his mouth off my cock and from the way his cheeks were puffed out I could tell he still had my cum in his mouth. He then leant forward and started kissing me, passing all my cum to me. I gratefully accepted my spunk from his mouth and being a greedy cum slut gulped it down.

We then began to passionately kiss as Arnold pulled my tracksuit bottoms off over my trainers. With my trackie bottoms off, he pushed my legs up so that my ass was exposed. He then bent down and dragged his jot wet tongue from the base of my spine, up between my ass cheeks, over my asshole, over the sensitive bridge between my ass and balls and then over my balls. A shiver of pleasure ran through me as Arnold did this.

He then repeated it several times, making me shiver and purr with pleasure each time. He then started homing in on my ass, circling his tongue all around the entrance to my ass and flicking his tongue over it, causing my pucker to quiver. Arnold then started stabbing his hot wet tongue in and out of my ass like a little cock. He really wormed his tongue deep inside my ass and caressed the walls with the tip. He soon had me panting and moaning like a bitch of heat as he prepped my ass for his manly cock.

Arnold tongue fucked my ass for ages and despite really enjoying the pleasure his tongue was orally lavishing on my ass I needed a big hot hard cock fucking it. "Fuck me, Arnold!" I begged as I looked down at his handsome face buried between my buttocks. I was eager to feel his thick manly cock fucking my tight teen ass rough, hard, and passionately. "Sure thing." He replied as he draped my legs over his shoulders. He then spat into the palm of his hand and rubbed it onto his cock.

Arnold shuffled up and I felt him press his knob against my ass ring. Our gazes locked and I saw the lust and passion in his face and eyes. I felt the pressure on my ass ring increase. It briefly resisted before popping open causing us both to moan with pleasure as Arnold's knob forced its way into my ass. As soon as his swollen knob had forced open my pucker he then powerfully slammed the rest of his thick, throbbing, manly cock ball deep inside me in one rough hard passionate thrust. "Fuck yes!" I cried out as Arnold powerfully impaled my teen ass on his cock. Arnold just grunted with pleasure as he felt my hot wet steamy tight ass wrap around his cock.

With his cock buried ball deep in me he launched straight into a fast, furious, rough hard fucking frenzy. No sooner had he bottomed out in my boy pussy than he was pulling his thick cock backwards, his retreating cock pulling out my ass lips as my ass sucked on it. He pulled all the way out, my asshole dilating, before slamming it back in, forcing open my ass lips and love chute. "Fuck yeah!" I cried as he impaled my ass on his cock again. I saw stars as I felt his knob force open my ass ring, causing a slight stinging, before he thrust the rest of his cock deep into me. His swollen knob forced open and caressed my ass walls as his thick shaft stretched and stimulated my sphincter. Due to the angle of our fucking position his knob slammed against my prostate hard, causing my teen cock to wildly throb and droll some more pre-cum into my soft pubes.

Arnold repeated this several times, pulling his manly cock all the way out of my ass before powerfully slamming it back in. Each time I cried out with pleasure and maybe a tinge of pain as this hunky man ploughed my teen boy cunt with his thick manly cock. There was a look of pure animal lust on Arnold's handsome face as he deep fucked my teen ass. He really wanted my ass to feel his cock and I sure was.

For a couple of minutes Arnold used the full 7 inches of his thick cock on my ass, pulling all the way out before slamming back in. This gave my ass lips a serious working over with the thick ridge of his hard meat forcing open, rubbing, and stretching my pucker. Then the thick shaft of his cock rubbed and pulled on my ass lips, as his knob caressed the walls deep in my ass. I was seeing stars and loudly groaning with pleasure at the rough hard pleasurable fucking I was getting.

After a couple of minutes Arnold stopped pulling his penis all the way out of my ass, but he continued to fuck me with equal passion and vigour. Now he would pull his cock back until the thick ridge of his knob butted up against the inside of my ass ring. Then he'd immediately slam it back in, rough and hard, until his sweaty pubed groin loudly and firmly slapped against my pert upturned ass.

My ass felt every powerful thrust of his manly cock. My ass lips were stretched and stimulated by his hot thick throbbing shaft as he see-sawed it in and out of my tight teen ass. His swollen knob forced open and caressed my soft wet ass walls and bumped my prostate, causing my cock to throb and drip pre-cum. His pubed groin slapped my ass with his pubes tickling my pucker. I drank in his strong sweaty musky arouse manly aroma and admired the look of pleasure and lust on his handsome face. I also felt his sweaty toned hairy chest muscles under my hands as I groped them and pinched his nipples until they were hard and red. Occasionally he would lean forward and passionately kiss me and I could taste my ass on his tongue.

I could tell from the way that Arnold was fucking me that I was in for a long hard rough passionate fuck, just how I like them. From my earlier fuck with Arnold I knew he could fuck very hard and could last for ages.

Arnold settled into a nice steady rhythm of deep hard passionate powerful thrusts, my ass feeling and savouring each one. We started talking dirty to each other. I would beg him to fuck me hard or tell him how good it felt having his thick manly cock fucking my tight teen ass. Whereas Arnold would call me names or tell my how good my young ass felt on his cock.

As he powerfully fucked me I drank in the strong heady erotic aroma of man on teen gay sex. There was the squelch of his cock thrusting my ass, which sucked on it with my sphincter wanking it. His erect dick forced open and caressed the sensitive walls of my ass and each inward thrust hit my prostate. Feeling his thick cock fucking my ass had my teen cock wildly throbbing and drooling pre- cum into my soft pubes. I flexed my ass muscles on his cock which increased the pleasure for both of us. His sweaty pubed groin slapped against my ass hard, his balls banging against it like a pendulum. I caressed his toned sweaty hairy chest muscles and pinched his hard-erect nipples as I watched the expressions of lust and passion on his handsome face.

I don't know how long Arnold kept up his passionate fucking for but it felt like ages and my ass was really beginning to glow and throb from the hard fucking it was taking. I could also feel the cum churning in my balls from the repeated hits of his swollen knob against my prostate as well as all the other mind blowing pleasurable sensations of being fucked up the ass hard by a hunky man 9 year my senior.

Then I felt him pick up the pace even more and the look on his face changed to that of pure carnal lust and passion. He started slamming his cock in and out of my tender well fucked ass even faster and harder, setting it on fire with increased pleasure.

I could tell that he was getting close to orgasm from the way he was fucking me and I could tell I wasn't far from the Ronald either. That changed when he suddenly grabbed my throbbing 6.5" uncut cock in his right hand. He began to furiously wank it, rapidly sliding his big strong rough hand up and down my smooth teen cock in a tight grip, peeling my foreskin back and forth over the sensitive ridge of my knob. This pleasure was added to by feeling his knob rubbing my ass walls and hitting my prostate hard as his shaft rubbed and caressed my swollen tender ass lips. I knew I wouldn't be able to take much more stimulation before I came but I fought back as long as I could which only increased the pressure.

We were both locked in a vicious circle of lust while at the same time trying to stave off our orgasm until after the other one had cum. My youthful horniness and bottom boy nature made it a losing battle for me. I only managed to hold out for a couple of minutes before being fucked rough and hard by a fit hunky 27-year-old guy as he rapidly wanked off my teen cook all got too much for me.

My ass lips were swollen, tender and on fire from the pleasure of a hot hard thick throbbing shaft rubbing against them. My ass was throbbing as his swollen knob forced open and caressed the walls. Having my prostate repeatedly rubbed was driving me wild with pleasure. The smell of gay sex and the sight of a sweaty hunky man fucking me all got too much.

I felt the pressure in my balls reach critical mass. My whole body tensed up and I arched my back which thrust my groin closer to my face due to the position and angle Arnold was fucking me in. As Arnold had a tight grip on my cock with one hand

and my hips with the other he just followed me and rammed his cock ball deep into my ass.

His swollen tool hitting my prostate was the trigger. With a loud cry hot teen spunk blasted out of my cock and hit me in the face and hungry mouth. This was followed by two more jets that squirted into my mouth and on my lips. I savoured the hot salty taste of my cum. Three more jets blasted out of my cock and splattered onto my tee shirt as wave after wave of intense sexual pleasure coursed through my body.

I was loudly moaning and groaning with pleasure as I orgasmed, my ass spasming uncontrollably around Arnold's thick thrusting cock. This sent him into a passionate fucking frenzy. He slammed his hot hard cock in and out of my wildly flexing ass really rough hard and fast. His rough hard fucking prolonged and intensified my orgasm which was slowly fading.

I was still in post orgasm glow, with Arnold still fucking me hard when I felt him slam his thick cock all the way in my ass. I saw Arnold arch his back as a look of intense lust and sexual pleasure spread across his handsome face. I felt his cock swell and throb in my ass as the first bolt of man spunk raced down his cock before I felt it explode out of the end and coat my tender ass walls. This jet was followed by several bigger powerful spurts of hot cum which filled up my ass.

We were both sweaty and loudly moaning as we each savoured intense sexual pleasure. I felt my throbbing tender well fucked ass filling up with his hot man spunk as the taste of my cum lingered in my mouth.

When Arnold shot the last of his load into my mouth he collapsed on top of me and I wrapped my legs around him. We both stayed like that, me sat on the edge of the chair with him knelt on the floor with my legs wrapped around him as we relished the post orgasm glow and caught our breath.

When we had recovered Arnold gingerly pulled out his spent cock, which was already starting to soften, from my tender ass. He then stood up and was about to walk away but I caught sight of his cock which was glistening in his cum and my ass juice.

Pure instinct kicked in and I grabbed his hips and pulled him to me. At the same time, I opened my mouth and sucked his cock into my mouth. As it was only semi hard I took it right in to the pubed base before tightly clamping my lips around it. I then began greedily sucking up and down, sucking off the tasty mix of my ass juice and his cum. There was no shit and it wasn't as gross as it sounds. "Yeah! suck my cock clean boy." Arnold moaned.

When I had sucked his cock clean I stood up and lifted his left arm up and then eagerly licked out his sweaty armpit and then I did the same with his right. "Come on let's go shower." Arnold said so I followed him to the bathroom as I enjoyed the taste of cum and ass juice mixed with Arnold's cum and sweat in my mouth.

5.

In the bathroom Arnold stepped into the shower and began soaping up as I stripped out of my socks, trackie top and cum splattered tee shirt. Unfortunately, there wasn't enough room for two so I just watched Arnold wash his hunky body through the steam and water droplet frosted glass. When he stepped out I stepped in and had a long luxurious shower.

After getting out I dried myself off and then, leaving my clothes discarded on the floor, went looking for Arnold naked. I found him in the kitchen wearing a pair of soccer shorts and making some sandwiches. "Jeeze where's your undies?" Arnold said looking at the naked 18-year-old boy stood in his kitchen doorway. "I don't wear any." I replied. Arnold eyed me up before saying "Go to the room at the right of the stairs and get a pair of shorts out of the top left-hand draw."

I went back upstairs and into the room he had told me. I walked over to the chest of draws and pulled open the left draw. There were socks, boxers, and soccer shorts in there and I pulled out a pair of white Umbro football shorts. As I pulled on the shorts I noticed a picture frame on top. In it were two very good-looking guys. One was blond with a really sexy face, killer smile, and dreamy light brown eyes. He looked about 23. The other guy looked a year or two older and had dark brown hair. His face wasn't as sexy as the blonds or Arnold's but he was still good looking.

When I got back into the kitchen I asked Arnold who the two guys were. I was under the impression that I had just been in Arnold's bedroom and the picture was of some friends. "Oh, that's Ronald & Ethan, my flat mates. I'm sure Ethan won't mind you using a pair of his shorts." "That was Ethan's room?" I asked confused. "No Ethan's & Ronald's. They are a couple and work the same site as me. They've gone to Brighton for a dirty weekend." "So, they are gay too?" I asked as I tried to get my head around it. "Yeah." "Cool." Was my reply. We then went back into the lounge and watched some TV and had our sandwiches.

After watching TV for an hour or so I started to feel horny again so I started rubbing Arnold's cock through the material of his shorts. In no time at all I had him boned up with his thick 7" cock throbbing in the confines of his satiny shorts. I was also boned up and was leaving a pre-cum stain on my borrowed shorts.

When Arnold was hard I fished out his cock and balls. I took time to admire his thick veiny cock before I bent forward, opened my mouth, and engulfed all 7 inches in one go. Once my nose was buried in his dense patch of brown pubes, I tightly clamped my lips around the base of his cock. I held his manhood in my mouth and felt it throb before I started pulling my hot wet mouth and tightly clamped ups up his thick veiny shaft. I pulled all the way up until I had just his swollen sensitive knob in my mouth which I began to eagerly suck as I swarmed my tongue all over it.

Arnold purred with pleasure I sucked away on his knob before lunging my hot wet mouth all the way down onto his cock again. I kept that up for a couple of minutes, alternating between deep throating his cock all the way down to the pubed hilt or pulling up to just suck and lick his knob.

I savoured the pleasure of having a man's cock in my mouth. The thickness of his shaft and its warm throbbing pulse. The smooth but veiny skin and the sponginess of his swollen knob. The taste of his pre-cum and the sight of his sexy cock.

As I sucked away on his manly cock my teen cock was wildly throbbing and drooling pre-cum into shorts that weren't mine. My tender cum filled ass was also quivering, eager for another good hard rough fucking.

I worked on his manhood for a good few minutes and I think Arnold thought I was going to suck him off but I had other ideas. As I carried on sucking his manhood I pushed my shorts off.

Now that I was naked and Arnold's cock was glistening with my saliva I straddled him so that my ass was inches above his cock. I reached behind and grabbed his throbbing saliva soaked cock in my right hand. I aimed it upwards as I positioned my ass over it, nestling his swollen knob up against my asshole.

I looked into Arnold's handsome face and sexy blue eyes. Without warning I just slammed my ass down. My ass lips parted and slid down over Arnold's swollen knob before tightly clamping around his thick shaft below the ridge of his knob. Without hesitation I thrust the rest of my hot tight wet ass down onto Arnold's 7-inch manly cock until my pert ass slapped against his pubed groin. We both let out a loan moan of pleasure as Arnold's cock filled my young ass. I felt all of his cock stretch and throb in my ass. My own teen cock was sandwiched between my smooth flat stomach and Arnold's slightly hairy washboard stomach.

"You horny little slut." Arnold gasped as he savoured having my hot tight teen boy cunt slammed onto and engulf his throbbing manhood. The look of shock on his sexy face as he had a horny boy impale himself on his cock was a classic. I held myself there for a while so that we could both rejoice in having his cock buried ball deep in my ass. I then lifted myself up and felt my tight love chute suck his cock and my ass lips get pulled out as I raised up his cock until I felt the thick ridge of his swollen knob butt up against the inside of my boy pussy.

Looking into his sexy face I then slammed my ass down onto his cock again. I felt his prick force open my love chute and stroke the walls of my tender cum filled ass as I impaled myself on his manhood. When I bottomed out on his cock I felt it throb and pulse in my ass, with his pubes tickling my ass ring. I gasped with the pleasure of forcing my ass onto his cock, savouring the wonderful feeling of having my tight teen ass full of thick throbbing man cock.

Arnold reached around and grabbed my ass to support it and aid in lifting it up and down his cock. I quickly settled into a steady rhythm of bouncing my hot, wet, tight, teen ass rough and hard up and down his manly cock. I'd pull up until just his swollen knob was inside my ass before I would slam it back down, all the way onto his hot hard throbbing cock until I had taken it in to the pubed hilt.

As I bounced up and down Arnold's cock my own cock rubbed against his firm hairy washboard stomach leaving snail trails of pre-cum. Each time I slammed my ass down onto his cock his knob would hit my prostate and cause me to dribble even more pre- cum.

As Arnold was sat on the sofa and I was knelt over him I was using my thighs to push myself up and down on his cock. Arnold also had a hold of my ass and was lifting me up and down. This meant my hands were free so I used them to grope his toned pecs, run my fingers through his chest hair and roughly tweak his nipples until they became red and puffy.

We were both loudly moaning and groaning with pleasure as I bounced my hot, wet tight teen boy ass up and down Arnold's hot, thick, throbbing manly 7-inch cock. As I rode it I flexed my ass muscles on it to increase the pleasure and stimulation for both of us. Each bounce had his thick shaft stretching and stimulating my ass ring. His swollen knob rubbed against my sensitive ass walls and hit my prostate. I felt every single thrust and it felt so dam good. "Yeah ride my cock pussy boy." Arnold moaned as I rode his manly cock like a cowboy.

With each bounce I started to feel hornier and even sluttier so I would slam my ass down onto his cock even harder. This just locked me into a vicious circle where I got hornier and rode his cock harder. My thighs were beginning to burn with the exertion of bouncing up and down and I could feel the cum boiling in my balls.

It was a shame there wasn't a mirror in the room because I would have loved to have watched myself bouncing up and down on this muscular guy's manly cock. Instead I concentrated on the look of pleasure on Arnold's handsome face and the sight and feel of his sweaty, hairy, hunky chest under my hands. On top of that, there was also the strong erotic smell of sex and the mind blowing good sensations of my tight ass repeatedly impaling itself onto his thick cock.

I rode Arnold for a blissful age before I felt the warning tingle rapidly rise in my cock as I felt the pressure in my ball increase. I fought back the urge to cum for as long as possible in order to prolong the pleasure for both of us. However, it was a losing battle.

I slammed my ass down onto Arnold's thick throbbing cock hard. I felt his shaft stretch and stimulate my ass ring a final time. chopper forced open and caressed my tender ass walls before hitting my prostate which was the final trigger.

His knob hit my prostate before I bottomed out on his cock. As soon as he hit my prostate I arched my back and let out a loud yelp of pleasure as a jet of hot jiz blasted out of my cock and splattered onto Arnold's hairy stomach. I then bottomed out on his cock, my smooth ass slapping against his pubed groin. I couldn't do anything but hold myself there as wave after waves of sexual pleasure coursed through my body as I orgasmed.

I was moaning like a bitch on heat as jet after jet of hot cum powerfully blasted out of my cock and splashed onto Arnold's stomach. As I orgasmed my ass spasmed uncontrollably around Arnold's throbbing cock.

I was too lost in my own pleasure but it was obvious that I had also brought Arnold to the brink of orgasm but I had stopped before he reached it. As my orgasm began to fade Arnold used his strength and grip on my ass to start rapidly lifting me up and down so that my spasming ass sucked up and down his cock.

I just went along for the ride as I was too exhausted to help him. Instead I was like a limp rag doll as he lifted my ass up and down on his cock. As he pulled my ass down he powerfully rammed his cock upwards, making sure he got maximum penetration and then he would pull back as he lifted my ass upwards. I was seeing stars from the intensity of my orgasm and the pleasure of Arnold's thick cock pounding my ass.

I weakly shot the last of my load onto his stomach as Arnold continued to bounce me up and down his cock for another couple of minutes. He was rapidly increasing the intensity and in my post orgasm daze I sensed he was getting close to orgasm so I started flexing my ass muscles on his cock harder.

Arnold's breathing became faster and hard before I felt him yank my ass down hard as he powerfully slammed his thick cock upwards. I felt his swollen knob force open my tender love chute and his thick shaft stretch my sensitive ass ring as he rammed it ball deep into my ass until his groin loudly slapped against my ass. With his manly cock buried deep in my teen ass I felt it swell and throb as he started powerfully blast jet after jet of hot man spunk deep into my ass.

We both loudly moaned and groaned with pleasure as Arnold filled my boy cunt up with his hot cum. I felt every throb of his cock and every jet of his cum splash against my ass walls.

When Arnold's orgasm finished I just collapsed on top of him and we both stayed like that was we got our breath, his cock slowly going limp in my ass. I then pulled myself off his cock and got down onto my knees between his muscular hairy thighs. I then started licking up my cooling cum from his stomach before greedily sucking his cock clean of my ass juice and his cum.

6.

After that we got dressed and went into town to do some window shopping. As we walked around town I felt his cum leaking out of my tender ass and forming a damp patch on the crotch of my trackies. I also had a slightly visible stain from where I had been leaking my pre-cum into them earlier. I felt proud to be seen walking around with such a fit hunky guy. We also went to check out the public toilet where we met but it was deserted so we went back to Arnold's place.

Even though Arnold had already fucked me twice already, I was still up for more and I wanted him to fuck me again. We both sat side by side on a sofa, watching TV. I was in my white Nike tracksuit and Arnold was wearing a pair of jeans and a tee shirt. I reached over and started rubbing the crotch of his jeans and I soon felt his cock stirring beneath. "You really are a horny devil slut!" Arnold jokingly said as I continued to rub his rapidly stiffening cock through the material of his jeans. I just answered by starting to undo his jeans.

Once his jeans were undone, I got off the sofa and knelt on the floor between his legs. I then pulled his jeans and boxer shorts down, Arnold lifting up his ass to aid me. I pulled them down exposing his thick throbbing manly cock and then his muscular tanned hairy legs. I pulled his jeans and boxers off before I started kissing, licking, and caressing my way up his legs. I savoured feeling his strong muscular hairy legs under my hands and tongue as I gradually drew closer and closer to his cock.

When I reached the top of his thighs I began to lap away at his big balls, causing him to purr with pleasure. I had no intention of sucking him for long as I was gagging for a good hard fucking but I needed to suck him enough to get him juiced up for my ass. As I licked away at his balls I admire the sight of his throbbing lightly tanned cock and drank in his manly smell.

After a couple of minutes, I dragged my hot wet tongue up the underside of his throbbing cock and over his swollen knob, lapping up the pearly drop of pre-cum. I then swarmed my tongue all over his knob before licking back down the sensitive underside to his balls.

I repeated this several times but sometimes I would lick up the underside and others up the left-hand side or right-hand side. I then concentrated on just swarming my tongue all over his swollen, sensitive knob and catching any pre-cum that leaked out of his cock. I savoured the taste of his pre-cum and the spongy feel of his knob on my tongue.

Then I kissed the tip of his cock before I relaxed my throat and began to push my moist lips down over his knob. I slid my lips down past the ridge of his knob where they tightly clamped around his throbbing shaft. I then carried on pushing my hot wet mouth down onto his cock. I kept going until I had all 7 throbbing inches in my mouth, his knob plugging the back of my throat and my nose buried in his pubes. "Fuck yeah! Swallow my cock." Arnold gasped as I deep throated him.

I then began to bob my hot wet sucking mouth up and down his cock. I pull my mouth up until the thick ridge of his knob butted up against the inside of my lips. I'd then lunge my mouth all the way down onto his cock until I had him all the way in my mouth.

My own cock was rock hard and leaking pre-cum into my already stained trackies from the pleasure of greedily sucking off this thick sexy cock. I spent several minutes deep throating his cock until it was glistening with my saliva and I had him hyper horny. I then pulled his tee shirt off over his head and exposed his tanned hairy washboard stomach and tanned, toned hairy chest.

Now that Arnold was sat totally naked and hard on the sofa, I twisted around and got into the doggy position on the floor in front of him. I then pulled down the back of my trackies so that I was still wearing them but with just my pale smooth pert ass on show. My cock was still wrapped in the satiny material of my trackies which felt so dam good on my cock.

I adjusted my position so that my head was twisted to the left with my right cheek and upper body pressed against the carpet. My ass was stuck up in the air as I was knelt on my knees with my upper body down on the floor. Now that I was in the position I wanted to be fucked. I said, "Come and fuck me hard." My ass was practically quivering in anticipation and felt sticky with cum from our earlier fucks. "You want me to rim you first." Arnold asked as he got on the floor behind me. "No,

I want it rough and raw." I begged as I psyched myself up for taking his thick manly cock up my tight teen ass.

I felt Arnold kneel behind me before I felt him rubbing his cock between my smooth buttocks as he searched out my asshole. He soon found it and I felt him press his swollen knob against my ass lips. As soon as he found the entrance he rammed his thick throbbing cock ball deep into my ass in one deep hard powerful thrust. I arched my back and cried out at the brutal penetration of my ass. My ass ring stung with being forced open so hard. This was continued as his thick shaft stretched and rubbed against my ass lips as his swollen knob forced open my love chute on its journey deep into my boy pussy.

Arnold pushed the whole of his dick inside my tight cum filled ass until his pubed groin loudly slapped against my smooth pert upturned ass. Arnold grunted with the pleasure of slamming his cock ball deep into the tight cummy ass of a teen boy and I groaned at having a man roughly invade my boy cunt.

Arnold only held his thick, throbbing 7-inch cock in my ass for the briefest of moment before he pulled it all the way out. My ass and sphincter sucked away at his retreating cock and my ass lips snapped closed when he pulled his swollen dick from my ass. I had no time to recover because as soon as he had pulled his cock all the way out of my ass, he slammed it back it.

"Fuck yeah!" I cried half in pain, half in pleasure. I felt his swollen knob force open my ass lips causing them to sting. Then his knob forced open and caressed the walls of my ass as he rammed it deep into me, his thick throbbing shaft stretching and stimulating my sphincter. His groin slapped against my ass as he buried all 7 throbbing inches of his cock into my ass, his pubes tickling my hole. "Yeah take my fucking cock kid!" Arnold cried as he pushed his cock all in my ass.

No sooner had he hit bottom then he was pulling all the way out of my ass again. My sphincter and love chute snapping shut as he totally withdrew his cock. Then he slammed it back in causing me to arch my back and cry out in pleasure/pain. Arnold repeated this several times, pulling his thick, throbbing meaty cock all the way out of my tight tender ass before slamming it back in ball deep.

My ass and pucker were beginning to get that dull throbbing, but pleasurable ache from being fucked so rough and hard. I was certainly enjoying being fucked so brutally but such a sexy hunky guy. I was loudly moaning and groaning with sexual pleasure and found that I was thrusting my ass backwards as Arnold slammed forward, making sure he got maximum penetration.

Arnold carried on using his thick manly cock on my ass for a few minutes. After that he stopped pulling it all the way out. Instead he would pull back until the thick ridge of his swollen cock butted up against my ass ring before he slammed it back into my ass ball deep.

My ass lips were on swollen and on fire from the rubbing they were getting from Arnold's thick, pounding shaft. His extended dick was rubbing my ass walls and hitting my prostate, which was making me drip pre-cum into my trackie bottoms. My buttocks were starting to sting from the repeated slapping of his groin against them. The room was filling up with the heady musky erotic aroma of gay sex. "Fuck yeah! Do me harder!" I cried out, totally swept up in the lust and passion of the moment. "Take it slut boy." Arnold growled as he rammed his manly cock up my ass again.

Arnold really went at fucking my ass, using all his strength and energy to pound his manly cock up my tight, tender, ass. He really wanted my boy cunt to feel that it had been fucked and he wasn't disappointing. Already my ass lips felt sensitive, swollen, and puffy. My ass was throbbing from the repeated pounding of his hot hard thick cock, my prostate stimulated to the max and the front of my trackies were soaked in my pre-cum. We were both loudly moaning and groaning in pleasure and talking dirty to him, me begging like the bottom slut I was and Arnold growling like the hunky top he was.

I was so incredibly turned on from the rough hard fucking Arnold was giving me. My hard cock was wildly throbbing in the satiny confines of my white Nike trackies bottoms. Each time Arnold slammed his cock into my ass, my cock throbbed which made my swollen sensitive knob rub against the satiny material of my trackie bottoms and when his knob hit my prostate I drooled more per-cum into them.

Arnold gave me a good hard rough pounding for ages, really setting my ass on fire with pleasure. I began to feel myself get hyper horny with the urge to cum rapidly building. "Rub my cock off through my trackies." I breathlessly gasped as he relentlessly pounded his thick manly cock ball deep my ass. Arnold complied by reaching around with his left hand and started rubbing my hard cock through the pre- cum soaked satiny material of my trackie bottoms. His right hand kept its tight grip on my hip which he was using to yank my ass backwards as he powerfully slammed his cock forward.

Each hard, powerful thrust of his thick manly cock had me moaning like a bitch on heat as his swollen knob rammed open my love chute, his thick shaft stretching and stimulating my ass ring. I felt the pressure of orgasm rapidly rising in my body and the repeated banging of his stiff dick on my prostate was driving me closer and closer to orgasm.

My whole being was centred on the wonderful feelings radiating from my very tender, sensitive, well fucked ass. It was throbbing with being fucked so long and hard and my pucker felt puffy and tender. My buttocks were glowing from the repeated slaps of Arnold's groin against them. His swollen knob rubbed the walls of my steamy hot wet tight ass and repeatedly hit my prostate.

On top of that pleasure was feeling of my throbbing sensitive cock wrapped in the satiny confines of my trackies and the tight grip of Arnold's hand. As he powerfully slammed his thick manly cock in and out of my ass he was furiously wanking my cock off, driving me ever closer to orgasm.

I desperate fought off the inevitable but it all got too much. I couldn't even warn that I was about to cum even if I wanted to. Suddenly the cum in my balls reached critical mass. I felt my hot spunk surge down my cock before it blasted out and into the satiny confines of my trackie bottoms. As they were tightly wrapped around my cock my hot cum bubbled around my swollen sensitive knob as I came, soaking the front of my trackies in my cum.

Wave after wave of intense sexual pleasure coursed through my body as I orgasmed. My orgasm was fuelled by the feeling of the satiny material of my trackies on my sensitive orgasming cock, the tight wanking grip of Arnold's hand, feeling his thick manly cock pounding my ass and hitting my prostate and the smell of gay sex. I was totally lost in my orgasm and the pleasure of being fucked hard by a hunky man, loudly moaning, and groaning with pleasure.

As I orgasmed my ass spasmed uncontrollably around Arnold's thick thrusting cock, which increased the sensation for both of us. This sent him off into a fucking frenzy with him pounding my ass faster and harder than ever. Now that I was orgasming my ass became even more sensitive and was really feeling the fucking it was getting but I knew there was no way Arnold could stop until he came so I just gritted my teeth and took the pounding.

Arnold was still fucking my ass really hard, when I felt him start to tense up as he raced towards climax. His cock was a blur as he rammed it in and out of my aching but satisfied ass and he was loudly groaning with the pleasure and exertion of fucking a teen boy's ass. I was still in my post orgasm glow but could still feel everything going on in my ass.

"Fuck yeah! Yeah! Oh fuck!" Arnold suddenly screamed as he rammed his cock all in my ass. I felt it swell, throb, and then pulse as it blasted jet after jet of hot cum into my already cummy, sensitive ass. He slammed his penis in and out of my ass using half strokes as he pumped his cum into me. I just moaned with pleasure as I felt my tender, well fucked ass filling with his man seed. I started flexing my ass muscles around his thick orgasming cock to drain him of cum.

Arnold had an intense powerful orgasm in my ass and when he finished cumming in me he couldn't help but collapse exhausted on top of me. We both stayed like that as we got our breath back and I felt his cock grow limp in my ass.

When we had recovered, Arnold pulled his cock from my ass, slapped it then went to the toilet. I got up and pulled up the back of my trackies. As I did so I saw the big obvious damp patch on the front of them and it felt good against my cock. I then sat on the sofa and waited for Arnold to return.

When he came back he got dressed again and we sat and watched some more TV as the cum patch dried on my trackies. Also, while I sat watching TV I felt Arnold's cum leaking out of my very tender but satisfied, cum filled ass and onto the crotch of my trackies.

About an hour after we had finished fucking it was time for me to go home. The front and crotch of my white trackies had dried but the felt crusty and my cum had left an obvious stain on the front. I would have to walk through town like that but that turned me on more than anything. I did get a few looks as I walked through town but and even a knowing smile off one guy but he was old and not my type so I didn't take it further.

7.

Although my relationship with Arnold, the hunky 27-year-old builder I met cottaging, was very new, it was also intense. I was thinking about him all day long. When I was not with him, I wanted to see him. When I was with him, I wanted to kiss him and have sex with him. I was dreaming of him every single day. Arnold and I didn't talk about our lives. All I knew about him was that he was a builder and all he knew about me that I go to university. Anytime we spent together was just sex.

Being a PhD student under a scholarship, I also had to teach. I went to teach my first lesson in Mathematics. There were only 20 students in this class, all part time students in an evening class. I stood in front of the class, introducing myself as a PhD student and their professor, even though I looked as a teenager. Then, I noticed Arnold sitting at the back. I tried to hide the surprise on my face but the surprise on his face was too obvious.

It was difficult to go through with the session and I rushed it as much as I could. Everyone started leaving the classroom, while a couple were asking me some questions. Arnold stayed seated until they were gone before he approached me. "So, you are a genius?! You never mentioned that!" He asked, "it is not something that I start up with, specially to someone I meet at a public bathroom" I replied, "and you never mentioned you were a student here?" I continued. "I have not told anyone else either"

It was very awkward between us, our dynamics had changed, I am not just the boy he is fucking anymore, I am his professor. He is not the guy I have been begging him to fuck me, he is my student. However, I couldn't help but admire Arnold. He had dark hair with a centre parting. His face was handsomely chiselled and tanned with piercing blue eyes and lush kissable lips. He was wearing a tight white tee shirt that hugged his hunky body perfectly. The sleeves were short so almost all his golden tanned muscular hairy arms were on show. He was also wearing a pair of tight light blue jeans. They really hugged his rock-hard buttocks and muscular legs. His jeans also showed off his package nicely too.

I knew that I was not supposed to be having sex with one of my students, but I was feeling really horny, and I was having a hard time controlling myself. My cock was very hard and obviously showing in my pants. "Wanna come to my place, professor?" Arnold said with a wink. "We are not supposed to be doing this." I replied. He got closer to me, grabbed my cock, and said, "I don't think your cock agrees."

We went back to Arnold's house where he grabbed us a couple of beers and we sat down on the sofa. It was quite hot and in no time at all my cock was rock hard again and tenting out my trousers, a pre-cum damp patch spreading across the blue material. From the occasional wiggle from Arnold, I guessed that he was hard too and knew his cock must be suffering in the tight confines of his jeans.

I got up and straddled him so that I was knelt over him with my ass pressed in his lap as I faced him. I ground my ass into his lap as I started kissing him. Arnold returned the kiss and we were soon passionately kissing away. I admired his handsome face as we kissed, our lips locked together and our tongues fencing.

As we kissed away, Arnold unbuttoned my shirt and pulled it off. Then he stuck his hands up my under-shirt and started caressing my flat smooth stomach and chest, toying with my nipples and making them go all hard and erect. He then pulled my under-shirt off over my head. By doing so we had to break our kiss. However rather than go back to kissing, Arnold pulled me towards him and started circling his tongue all over my right nipple. I purred with pleasure as I felt his tongue circling my nipple, making goose bumps come out all around it and make me nipple harder. He then started flicking his tongue all over it before he took it between his teeth and started gently chewing and tugging on it. "Harder." I begged, really wanting him to work over my nipple. Arnold obeyed and started chewing and tugging on my nipple harder until it went all red, puffy, and hyper sensitive.

He licked, sucked, tugged, and chewed on my right nipple before he moved over to my left. He did exactly the same, starting off with gentle licks and ending up chewing and tugging it until it was a red a swollen as my right nipple. He then pulled me close to him and we started to passionately kiss, his tongue forcing its way into my mouth and battling my tongue into submission.

As we kissed, I began to pull up his tight white tee shirt. When I got it to his head we broke off our kiss. I looked down to admire Arnold's sexy tanned toned hairy chest and washboard stomach as I pulled his tee shirt off over his head. Now that he was bare-chested I was fully able to admire it. As I looked at it I ran my hands all over it feeling the muscles and chest hairs under my fingers. I knew that what we were doing was completely wrong by the university rules, and I would be in extreme trouble if anyone finds out, but couldn't resist myself around him, and I then lent forward and began to kiss him.

I only kissed him briefly before I lifted his left arm exposing his hairy arm pit. I immediately dove in and drank in its musky sweaty smell before I started greedily licking it out, tasting its saltiness while Arnold moaning with pleasure.

Once I'd licked it clean I licked over to his left nipple, dragging my tongue through his chest hairs. When I reached his nipple, I circled my tongue around it and felt goose bumps forming under my tongue. This also made his dark brown nipple become erect so I started flicking my tongue over it. I then gently gripped it between my teeth before I started chewing and tugging away at it. I knew Arnold liked rough nipple play as much as I did so I was quite rough with it, soon making it all red swollen and puffy.

I then dragged my tongue through his brown chest hairs to his right nipple. I did the same to this too. As I licked, sucked, and chewed his right nipple I was roughly pinching his left saliva soaked nipple. When I had it nice and swollen I kissed and licked my way over to his right arm. I lifted it up and exposed his hairy pit, which I dove in and licked out as I drank in its musky erotic smell.

After licking out his right armpit I licked back to between his hairy pecs. I then dragged my tongue down the trail of hair leading from between his pecs and down the centre ridge of his washboard stomach to the waistband of his jeans. As I moved down his body I slid down so that when I reached the waistband of his jeans I was knelt on the floor in between his legs.

Now that I was level with his groin I could see that he was hard, with the outline of his thick manly cock down the left leg of his jeans. I started rubbing his hard cock through the material of his jeans as I looked up at his handsome face. After a while I began to undo his jeans and pulled them down. Arnold lifted his ass off the sofa to aid me. As I pulled them down I exposed his tight white boxer-briefs which showed off the outline of his thick cock wonderfully. As I pulled them further down, I exposed his golden tanned muscular sexy hairy thighs and then lower legs.

I pulled them off his legs and took off his socks too. I then began slowly kissing, licking, and caressing my way up his very sexy muscular hairy legs. When I reached his bulging briefs I nuzzled my face against them and felt the warm throbbing pulse of his manly cock through them. I then gripped the material tightly around his cock and wrapped my lips around the top inch or so of his cock. With his covered swollen knob in my mouth I began to suck and lick it, soaking the material of his boxers in my saliva. I had his covered cock in my left hand and I was using my right hand to caress his muscular left thigh or to caressing his stomach and chest, running my fingers through the hairs.

As I sucked his rigid tool through the material of his briefs the taste of his pre- cum started filtering through. When it hit my tongue I just knew I had to taste it fresh from the source. I hooked my fingers under the waistband of his boxers and started pulling them down. First, I exposed his dense patch of brown pubes. Then the base of his lightly tanned thick meaty cock came into view. As I pulled his boxers further down more of his sexy cock came into view. Soon I had all of it exposed and I admired it as I pulled his boxers the rest of the way off his hunky legs.

I took in the sight of his big hairy balls nestled between his very toned hairy thighs. His cock was rock hard and twitching against his left thigh. It looked so sexy and suckable that my mouth was watering. I firmly gripped his cock in my left hand and felt its warm throbbing pulse and thick meaty girth. I gave it a couple of wanks, peeling his foreskin back and forth over his swollen knob. As I did so I saw a drop of pre-cum forming at the tip. I leant forward and licked it up, savouring the taste. I then began swarming my tongue all over his swollen sensitive knob. I flicked my tongue over the tip to lick up any tasty pre-cum. I licked the sensitive underside where his foreskin joined or I'd lick all around his swollen helmet, savouring its taste and sponginess.

As I licked away on Arnold's knob I heard him moan with pleasure and he started running the fingers of his right hand through my shaggy hair. My own cock was rock hard and leaking pre-cum into my trackie bottoms, which by now must have had a big pre-cum stain on the front.

I spent awhile just licking his firm knob before I kissed the tip and slid my mouth down onto it. My moist lips slid down his flared knob and over its ridge, before tightly clamping around his thick shaft just below his knob. With his knob in my mouth I began greedily sucking away at it as I swarmed my tongue all over it. As I sucked and licked away on his swollen knob I heard him moan with pleasure, felt his cock throb and pulse in my hand and tasted the pre-cum leaking from the tip. I also drank in his musky manly aroused aroma and admired his sexy cock.

I gave his swollen sensitive knob a good working over before I relaxed my jaw and throat and started sinking my mouth down onto his cock. As I took more of his manhood into my cock sucking mouth my lips caressed down his thick meaty veiny shaft as I flicked the underside with my tongue. I worked my mouth all the way down his cock until my nose touched his pubes, with his firm dick plugging my throat and all 7 inches throbbing in my mouth. "Oh yeah choke on my cock professor." Arnold moaned as I started flexing my throat muscles on his knob as I caressed his muscular hairy thighs with my hand. I was glad that I could show my cock sucking abilities on this sexy hunky man.

When the urge to breathe kicked in I pulled my mouth back up his cock, caressing it with my tightly clamped lips and flicking it with my tongue as I sucked up it. I pulled up until I just had his swollen sensitive knob in my mouth, which I sucked and licked away on before sliding my mouth back down onto his cock. Again, I sank my mouth all the way down until I can feel his pubes on my nose.

I then broke into a steady rhythm of bobbing my hot wet sucking mouth over his thick sexy cock, wanking it with my lips, caressing it with my tongue and sucking it. When I pulled up and just had his swollen knob in my mouth I sucked it and swarmed my tongue all over it to lap up his tasty per-cum. All the while Arnold was moaning with pleasure. He moans and words of encouragement showed that I was doing an excellent job as did the throbbing of his cock and the amount of pre-cum he was leaking into my mouth.

I was really enjoying myself sucking away on his cock. I felt the hot thick throbbing meatiness of his cock in my mouth. I drank in his slightly sweaty musky manly aroused aroma. I savoured the taste of his pre-cum as I felt his muscular hairy thighs under my caressing hands. Arnold was giving me free reign on his cock so that I was in full control of the blow job. Some of the time I was deep throating all 7 inches so that I had my nose buried in his pubes with his swollen cock plugging the back of my throat where I'd work the muscles on it. Others I'd just have his swollen knob in my mouth which I would strongly suck on as I swarmed my tongue all over, paying particular attention to the sensitive underside where his foreskin joined. If I wasn't doing any of those I would be sucking it half way in or licking up and down it like a lollipop.

I sucked away on Arnold's manly cock for ages, turning us both on but he had other ideas. "Jeez you sure know how to suck cock, professor!" Arnold gasped. "But I'm so in the mood to fuck you now." I pulled my mouth off his saliva soaked cock and said, "You read my mind." "Kneel on the edge of the sofa." He said. I did as he said and knelt on the edge of the sofa, with my hands on the back to support myself. Arnold stood up behind me and I felt his caress and grope my firm pert ass through the tightly stretched material of my trousers. I then felt him rubbing his hot hard saliva soaked cock up and down the crack of my covered ass.

Arnold then hooked his fingers under the waistband and pulled them down. First, he exposed my pale pert ass, before pulling them down my subtly toned lightly haired thighs to my knees. When he got to my keens I lifted up my left knee and then my right so that he could get my trousers past them. He then continued to pull them off, taking my socks with them. I was now knelt naked on his sofa, lent forward, and using my hands to support my weight on the sofa back. Arnold then began to caress and grope my naked ass and I enjoyed feeling his big rough strong hands all over my peachy young ass.

Arnold played with my ass for a bit and then I felt him kneel behind me and with a hand on each buttock he parted them. Next, I felt his warm breath and his hot wet tongue on my ass. I felt him lick over the sensitive area where my balls joined, up between my pert buttocks, over my ass ring making it quiver and then up and over the base of my spine. I broke out in goose bumps of pleasure and let out a sigh of delight. Arnold then repeated this a few times, giving my ass long slow firm licks form my balls to the base of my spine. Each one made me shiver and sigh with pleasure and had my ass ring quivering.

Arnold then started homing in on my ass. His licks became shorter and more concentrated around my asshole. Soon he was just circling his hot wet tongue around the tight, sensitive ring of muscle guarding my ass. His warm breath washing over it also had me tingling with pleasure. I could feel my pucker quivering uncontrollably as Arnold circled his tongue around it. He then started flicking his tongue over it which made me start purring with pleasure more loudly.

Gradually Arnold increased the oral pleasure on my sphincter. He went from circling his tongue around it to flicking over it. Now he was starting to force his tongue into my ass, stabbing it in and out like a little cock. When he worked it inside my ass he wiggled and wormed it about so that he got it as deep into my funky ass as he could.

I let Arnold tongue fuck my ass for a couple of minutes before it got too much for me. It was nice having him tongue fucking and licking my ass but all it was doing was fanning the yearning for his thick manly cock to fuck it hard and raw. "Fuck me. please." I begged as he wormed his tongue into my ass again. Arnold ignored my request for a bit which made me want his cock even more, but then I felt him pull away from my ass and saw him walk over to the sideboard where he opened a draw and pulled out a tube of lube.

Arnold then walked around so that he was stood in front of me, his cock right next to my face. Out of natural cock sucking bottom boy instinct I opened my mouth and took his thick throbbing manly cock inside and tightly clamped my lips around it about half way down. I then sucked and licked it bobbing my hot wet sucking mouth up and down the top half of his cock as he squirted some lube onto his hand. When he was ready he pulled his cock from my mouth and lubed it up. I watched transfixed as he slid his hand up and down his thick meaty manly cock.

When it was lubed up he came back around and stood behind me. He ran his hand up and down my downy haired ass crack, smearing the remaining lube on to my quivering ass ring. I then felt him rub his hot hard cock up and down my crack as he searched out my hole. When he found, it I felt him start to press his swollen knob against my ass ring. He increased the pressure and my pucker briefly resisted before his firm cock forced it open and popped inside. A grunt escaped from me and a groan came from Arnold as my tight ass lips slid down over his flared knob. They pasted over the ridge before tightly clamping around his shaft. His swollen sensitive knob now had the steamy hot wet tight walls of my ass wrapped around it.

As soon as his knob breached my ass' defences he carried on forcing the rest of his thick meaty cock into my teen boy ass. His hot thick veiny shaft stretched and stimulated my ass lips as he forced more and more of his cock into me. His swollen knob forced open and caressed the walls of my tight ass and I flexed my muscles on his invading cock. Arnold forced all 7 inches of his manhood into my ass until his densely pubed groin pressed up against my smooth buttocks.

He held his cock in my ass and jerked it about so we could both savour the pleasure. I savoured having my ass feeling so full and stretched by 7 inches of hot thick meaty man cock. He then started pulling his cock back and my ass and pucker sucked at it as he did so. He pulled back until the ridge of his swollen knob butted up against the inside of my ass ring. He then slammed his cock back into my ass ball deep. His densely pubed groin loudly slapped against my ass. His thick meaty shaft stretched and stimulated my tight ass ring as his swollen chopper forced open and caressed the walls of my love chute. I grunted with the force that he had used to slam his cock into me and he groaned with the pleasure of roughly invading a teen boy's ass.

Arnold quickly settled into a rough hard passionate fucking rhythm. He fucked me with long deep hard powerful thrusts of his cock, using all 7 inches on my ass making sure I really felt every inch. I was groaning with pleasure, really relishing the rough hard fucking this hunky guy was giving me. My ass was on fire with the friction and pleasure of having a thick cock repeatedly thrust hard up it. My ass ring was also glowing from having his shaft stretch and rub it, as his big hairy balls banged against my smaller balls. His densely pubed groin was loudly and firmly slapping against my pert upturned peachy ass. Each thrust of his cock had his large swollen knob banging against my prostate, causing my rock-hard cock to dribble even more pre-cum over the sofa back.

As he fucked me I flexed my ass muscles on his thick pounding cock. I clenched them tight when he forced his cock in and relaxed when he pulled out. This increased the stimulation and pleasure for both of us. His rough hard fucking soon had me delirious with pleasure. "Oh yeah Arnold fuck me harder!" I cried out, eager for him to fuck my ass raw. I drank in the heady erotic smell of man on teen gay sex and waves of pleasure radiated out form my roughly fucked ass.

"Yeah take my rod little slut." Arnold groaned as he sank his manly cock into my ass again. He had a very firm grip on my hips and was using it to yank my ass backwards onto his forward thrusting cock, making sure he got greatest penetration. I was throwing my head about in pleasure as I took a serious fucking from Arnold. My ass was getting tender and sore but in that really good way that lets you know you are being fucked great.

8.

He lived in a house with two other gay builders. So far, I had only seen a photo of his two housemates but they were both hot.

The younger of the two was called Ethan and he was 23. I thought he was the sexiest, even sexier than Arnold. He had light blond hair and a really sexy lightly tanned face, with dusting freckles over his nose. He had deep blue dreamy eyes and real lush kissable lips. That was all I could tell from the photo as it was just of his face and his boyfriend's face.

Ronald was Ethan's boyfriend and he was 25. He wasn't as sexy as Arnold or Ethan but he was still hot. He had a mean look that was quite sexy. He had short dark brown hair with a slightly mean chavy face with bluey grey eyes. It was hard to describe. It was an attractive face but not in the usual sense of the word.

We'd been fucking away for about 10 minutes, both totally lost in the lust and passion of the moment and oblivious to everything except the carnal pleasure of our union. However, that was soon shattered when we heard someone say, "Jeez look at them go." "Arnold's sure giving the kid a seeing too." Someone else added. Both Arnold and I looked over to where the voices had come from. Ronald & Ethan were stood in the doorway to the living room. At first, I was shocked at being caught in such an intimate yet compromising position. Here I was kneeling naked on a sofa, being shafted up the ass by a hunky guy and being discovered by his two housemates. I felt myself going red.

Arnold however seemed unfazed by it and if anything started to fuck my ass even harder and faster than before. For a while no one said anything. Arnold carried on fucking me like a whore and all I could do was take it as his two housemates watched on. "We may as well join them." Ronald said and with that both Ronald & Ethan walked into the room. It was now that I began to wonder if this was a set up and they had planned it all along. If it wasn't planned why didn't Ronald & Ethan go to their room and have fun there. Instead they stood nearby and started passionately kissing each other. I must admit it was very erotic watching two sexy guys snogging away.

As Ronald & Ethan kissed away they started taking each other's clothes off. Ronald's tee shirt was the first to come off. He had a very toned pale body with only his forearms having much colour. He had a pale smooth washboard stomach and nicely shaped pale chest, with a few dark wispy hairs between his pecs. His arms were also nicely toned but not as muscular as Arnold's.

Then Ronald pulled off Ethan's tee shirt. Ethan was as golden tanned as Arnold was. He also had a nicely shaped body but although he was as bulky as Ronald he didn't have quite the definition. However, it was still as sexy tanned lickable body. Ethan had a few dark blond hairs around his big brown chewable nipples and a dusting between his pecs. He also had a trail of blond brown hairs just above his navel which lead down into the waistband of his jeans. I admired both of their bodies and thought how sexy and lickable they looked.

Ronald and Ethan then began undoing their jeans at the same time. While all this was going on Arnold was still fucking me senseless, ramming his thick meaty manly cock up my tight ass, setting it on fire with pleasure. We were both loudly moaning and groaning with pleasure as we watched Ronald & Ethan strip off. I watched as they pushed down each other's jeans. They both had sexy legs. Ethan's were golden tanned, nicely shaped, and hairy, covered in dark blond hairs. Ronald's were pale with more definition but not as hairy, instead being covered in fine dark hairs.

I then watched with avid interest as they pushed down each other's boxers. They were both hard and erect and my eyes were immediately drawn to their cocks. Ethan's cock was as tanned as the rest of him. Like Arnold, Ethan had an all over body tan. His cock looked to be about 7 inches long, of average thickness and uncut. He had big balls that were covered in dark blond pubes. Overall, Ethan looked very sexy naked. Ronald on the other hand had the biggest cock I had seen up until that point. It was as thick as Leroy's cock but a bit longer. Leroy had an 8-inch cock, which he'd occasionally fuck me with. Ronald's cock looked to be 8.5 to 9 inches long. It was also thick, veiny, pale, and circumcised.

Both Ronald & Ethan looked very sexy naked. Once they'd shed their clothes, they came over to our sofa. Ethan sat on the sofa next to me and Ronald knelt on the floor in front of him. I twisted my head around so I could watch the action. I saw Ronald grab the tube of lube Arnold had discarded on the floor. I then watched struck as Ronald started greasing up his impressive cock. It looked even bigger and sexier now that I was seeing it closer and I started to envy Ethan who would soon be skewered on the end of it.

When Ronald had his cock lubed Ethan lifted his sexy tanned hairy legs. I then watched as Ronald moved forward, aiming his big thick sexy cock at Ethan's ass. He pressed his large swollen cut knob against the entrance to Ethan's ass. It saw it briefly resist before giving way and Ronald's swollen knob popped inside. Ethan let out a grunt as his boyfriend breached his ass. His grunt turned into a sigh as Ronald thrust the rest of his thick meaty 8.5-inch cock ball deep into his ass. The look of pleasure on Ethan's sexy face was priceless and made me envy him even more.

As soon as Ronald bottomed out in Ethan's ass he pulled back before launching into a steady fast hard fucking pace. I watched mesmerised, seeing Ronald's big cock thrusting in and out of Ethan's tanned ass. Soon their moans and groans were joining mine and Arnold's. It was so erotic watching Ronald fucking Ethan as Arnold fucked me.

We fucked like that for a few minutes when Ethan leaned over, moving his head between the sofa back and my body. I was half lost in the pleasure from being fucked so hard by Arnold but I did look down and saw Ethan moving closer and closer to my raging cock. I saw him open his mouth and engulf my cock in it. I let out a moan of pleasure as Ethan tightly wrapped his lips around my shaft about two thirds of the way down. I felt the wet warmth of his mouth engulf my cock, sending waves of pleasure down it, joining the pleasure radiating out from my hard-fucked ass.

With my cock in his mouth Ethan started strongly sucking and licking it. He then started bobbing his hot wet sucking mouth up and down my cock, wanking it with his lips and caressing it with his tongue. The sight of his tanned sexy handsome face sucking on the end of my cock looked so dam hot. Just the sight alone was enough to have the cum boiling in my balls, let alone the actual physical pleasure he was orally lavishing on my cock.

I couldn't believe what was happening. One minute I'm being fucked by my student, a hunky 27-year-old guy and the next I have a 23-year-old sucking me off at the same time as he's being fucked by a well hung 25-year-old. My ass was on fire with the pleasure of being fucked rough and hard by Arnold's thick cock. His shaft was stretching and stimulating my ass ring. His swollen knob was forcing open and caressing the walls of my ass and hitting my prostate. His pubed groin was firmly slapping against my pert ass as he bottomed out, his balls banging against mine.

On top of that pleasure there was now the pleasure of having Ethan sucking on my cock. I felt the wet warm heat of his mouth tightly clamped around my cock, strongly sucking it, and caressing it with his tongue. I felt his lips rubbing up and down my cock as he sucked away. Looking down at his sexy face slurping on the end of my cock was so erotic. I was loudly moaning and groaning with the intense sexual pleasure of it all.

We were like that for several more minutes, Arnold fucking my ass rough and hard as Ethan sucked me off. I alternated between watching Ethan sucking on my cock and watching Ronald slam his big thick meaty cock in and out of Ethan's ass. It all started to get too much for me though. The visual pleasure of seeing Ronald fuck Ethan as Ethan sucked me off was added to by the physical pleasure of Ethan sucking me off as Arnold fucked me senseless. The repeated thrusts of Arnold's hot hard thick throbbing 7-inch cock in and out of my ass was driving me mad with pleasure, especially as each thrust resulted in my prostate being bumped by his swollen knob. My cum was boiling in my balls from the stimulation Arnold was giving my prostate and Ethan was orally lavishing on my cock. I knew I wouldn't be able to hold out for much longer.

I felt the pressure rapidly building in my balls and felt the warning tingle. "I'm going to cum." I gasped to warn Ethan. He responded by sucking on my cock even harder. He pulled his mouth back so that he just had my sensitive knob in his mouth. As he started to suck it harder he flicked his tongue over the sensitive underside where my foreskin joined. This was too much for me especially when Arnold slammed his cock deeper into my ass again, his firm penis hitting my prostate.

I arched my back and cried out with pleasure as I felt my first powerful jet of cum blast out of my cock and into Ethan's mouth. I heard Ethan muffle a moan of pleasure as I coated his tongue with my cum. 6 more jets of diminishing power and amount rapidly followed the first jet. I could feel my cum bubbling around my cock so I knew Ethan was letting it pool in his mouth. Wave after intense wave of sexual pleasure radiated out from my cock and balls as I spunked up in the hot wet sucking confines of this sexy guy.

As I orgasmed my ass spasmed uncontrollably around Arnold rapidly thrusting cock, this sent him into a fucking frenzy. He started pounding my ass even faster and harder than before. When I shot the last of my load into Ethan's mouth he pulled it off my cock. I looked down at his sexy face and saw him swilling my spunk about in his mouth and then I saw him swallow it. Now that he had swallowed my load he moved his head from under me so he could look at Ronald fucking him.

From the way Arnold was rapidly and powerfully slamming his cock in and out of my ass, I could tell that he was getting very close to orgasm too.

His breathing was also laboured and his moans and groans were getting more frequent. My ass was now on fire with pleasure overload. My orgasm had just made it even more sensitive. My ass ring was glowing from the friction of his thick shaft rapidly rubbing against and stretching it. His swollen knob was forcing open and rubbing the tender walls of my ass. My buttocks were mildly stinging from the repeated slaps of his groin against them. Also, now that I was coming down from my orgasm high I was starting to flex my ass muscles on his thrusting cock harder and faster.

Arnold fucked me rough fast and hard for another couple of minutes before I felt him slam his cock into my battered ass one last time. I felt it swell throb and pulse as it started blasting jet after jet of hot cum deep into my ass. Arnold loudly grunted and groaned with pleasure as he spunked up in my ass. At the same time, I moaned with the pleasure of having a hunky guy cumming in my ass. As he came he bucked up against me as if trying to ram more of his cock up my ass, even though it was already buried up to the pubed hilt.

I heard and could feel that Arnold had a big powerful orgasm and I could feel his hot cum up me. When he finished spunking up in me he held his cock deep inside me for a bit before pulling out. My ass felt tender but very satisfied. Arnold then headed off to the toilet for a piss and to clean his cock. That left me alone with Ethan and Ronald. I watched as Ronald fucked his boyfriend really hard and it was obvious they were both enjoying it and seemed to relish having me watching them. It was then that I saw Ethan's cock.

I saw Ethan's tanned hard cock throbbing and bouncing on his tanned lightly haired stomach. I could see snail trails of pre-cum all over his stomach as Ronald's hard fucking of his ass made his cock bounce about. It looked so dam sexy and suckable. Out of pure cock sucker instinct, I leant over and grabbed Ethan's sexy cock so that it was inches from my face. "Go on suck him off. I'd love to see your cute face sucking on my boyfriend's cock." Ronald moaned as he slammed his cock into Ethan's ass again. I didn't need to be told twice.

I pulled Ethan's foreskin back and felt the smoothness of his cock and its throbbing hardness. I took time out to admire his sexy hard cock up close. He had a dense patch of dark blond pubes which ran from his groin and up his lower stomach. His cock was golden tanned, uncut and 7 inches long with a pink red swollen knob. His balls were big, tanned and covered in the same dark blond pubes. I moved in and licked up the pearl of pre-cum from the tip and savoured its taste. I then started swarming my tongue all over his swollen spongy knob, savouring its taste and feel on my tongue. Ethan let out a moan but I didn't know if that came from me licking his knob or Ronald slamming his big cock up his ass.

As I licked away on Ethan's knob, I had a bird's eye view of Ronald's big thick meaty cock slamming in and out of Ethan's ass. When Ronald pulled back I saw Ethan's pink brown ass lips get sucked out. Ronald would pull back until just his swollen cut knob was in Ethan's ass, before he powerfully rammed the rest of his 8.5" cock ball deep into Ethan's ass. I sure was envious of Ethan being fucked by such a big thick sexy cock and I wished I was in his place. From the moans and groans Ethan was making he sure was enjoying it.

After giving Ethan's knob a good licking I kissed the tip before I started sliding my lips down his flared knob. They pasted over the ridge before tightly clamping around his shaft below the ridge. With his swollen knob in my mouth I began to greedily suck it as I circled my tongue all over it. As I did so I felt him drooling loads of tasty pre-cum onto my tongue. From the state of his stomach and the taste in my mouth he was a real pre-cum leaker. "Fuck yeah that feels so good." Ethan gasped and again I wondered if he was talking about my cock sucking abilities of Ronald's ass fucking abilities.

For a while, I just sucked on Ethan's knob as I watched Ronald thrust his big thick pale veiny cock in and out of Ethan's tanned stretched ass. I then relaxed my throat and jaw and started forcing my hot wet sucking mouth down onto Ethan's sexy tanned 7-inch cock. I forced my mouth all the way down it until I had my nose buried in his dark blond pubes with his erect knob plugging the back of my throat, with all 7 inches of his cock throbbing in my mouth. I flexed my throat muscles on his knob before I pulled my mouth back up his cock. As I pulled my mouth up his sexy tanned cock I sucked it and flicked my tongue along the underside as my lips wanked it.

I was busy slurping away on Ethan's hot cock when Arnold returned. "Professor here is a really cock slut here." Ronald said as he slammed his big cock into Ethan's ass again. I was surprised that he knew I was a professor, but I was so lost in my sluttiness. "What do you expect? I met him cruising a public toilet." Arnold said as he watched me greedily sucking on his flat mate's cock.

The three of us soon found a steady rhythm. I was bobbing my sucking mouth over Ethan's sexy tanned cock as Ronald slammed his big thick cock in and out of Ethan's tanned ass. From the loud and frequent moans and groans of pleasure coming from Ethan he sure seemed to be enjoying having a cock hungry lad suck his cock as a hunky well hung guy fucking his ass.

I was also getting a great deal of pleasure from it. There was the highly erotic sight of Ronald's pale thick meaty cock slamming in and out of Ethan's tanned ass, the colour contrast of pale cock and tanned ass looked so good. I also saw his thick cock pulling out Ethan's pink brown ass lips, when he pulled back, only to force them back in when he slammed forward. I also drank in the heady musky sweaty aroused aroma of two sexy guys engaged in passionate gay sex. There was also the sight of Ethan's sexy tanned hard cock, as well as the feel of it rubbing against my tightly clamped lips and licking tongue. It also tasted delicious as it drooled loads of pre-cum onto my tongue. I was really doing my best to impress Ethan with my cock sucking abilities and I seemed to be succeeding.

Sometimes I would deep throat all 7 inches of his cock and work my throat muscles on his swollen knob, as I had my nose buried in his dark pubes. Other times I just had his swollen knob in my mouth which I greedily sucked away at as I swarmed my tongue all over it. Then I might lick up and down it like a lollipop before taking it back into my mouth.

Ronald then started fucking Ethan even faster and harder than before, really slamming his big thick cock up his ass. I guessed that Ronald was getting close to orgasm and had slipped into the pre-orgasm fucking frenzy. This also set Ethan off. He started moaning louder and more frequent and begging for Ronald to fuck him harder. I also got in on the act by starting to only take half of his cock into my mouth but suck it faster and harder.

I sucked Ethan's cock harder and faster as Ronald fucked his ass faster and harder. "I'm going to cum." Ethan gasped. I quickly pulled my mouth up so that I just had his cock in my mouth. I strongly sucked away at it as I flicked my tongue on the sensitive underside where the foreskin joined. Ronald also fucked him harder. I then felt Ethan's cock swell and throb in my hand as it started powerfully blasting jet after jet of hot thick tasty cum into my mouth. I let his hot jiz pool in my mouth around his cock. He fired 6 big powerful jets of cum into my mouth, totally coating my tongue in delicious cum. I savoured the taste as I flicked my tongue on the sensitive underside of his knob.

Ethan loudly moaned and groaned and shook and shivered with pleasure as he spunked in my cock and cum hungry mouth. As he came Ronald carried on fucking his ass hard. When Ethan stopped cumming I swallowed his spunk before gently sucking on his spent cock.

Almost as soon as Ethan finished cumming Ronald moaned that he was going to cum. I saw Ronald slam his big cock ball deep into Ethan's ass before he started shuddering and bucking against Ethan. I could tell that he was firing his hot jiz deep into Ethan's ass. Ethan's moans and the look of pleasure on his sexy face confirmed this.

Ronald kept his cock ball deep in Ethan's ass for a bit after he finished orgasming. Then he slowly pulled it out and I watched fascinated as more and more of his thick cock came into view. When he finally pulled it all out, it was shiny with his cum and Ethan's ass juice. There was no sign of shit and before I knew what I was doing I had Ronald's big slimy cock in my mouth and I was sucking it clean. "Fuck, he is horny." Ronald gasped as I took his cock into my mouth. I savoured the saltiness of his jiz and the earthiness of Ethan's ass juice. I spent about a minute sucking him clean before he pulled his cock from my mouth as it had become hyper sensitive.

"If you liked the taste of that, lick out Ethan's ass." Ronald half commanded as he moved out of the way. I took up Ronald's old position and knelt on the floor in front of Ethan. Ethan had his hands behind his knees holding his legs back. I admired the backs of his sexy hairy tanned thighs and his firm toned ass. His ass was covered in fine lighter blond hairs with dark hairs in his crack. I saw that his pink brown ass ring now looked redder and more swollen. I also saw a drop of Ronald's cum at the entrance. I dove straight in a dragged my tongue from the base of Ethan's spine, up between his buttocks, over his ass hole collecting the cum from there and then over the sensitive bridge. I then went back to his hole and circled my tongue around the tight ring of muscle before I started stabbing my tongue in and out of Ethan's ass as I tried to lick Ronald's cum out of it. I was drunk with hormones, the heady sweaty aroused smell of Ethan and the earthy taste of his ass juice mixing with the saltiness of Ronald's cum.

I spent a couple of minutes tongue fucking Ethan's ass before I stopped as I could sense Ethan's position was starting to get uncomfortable for him despite whatever pleasure he might be getting from me tongue fucking his cummy ass. "Thanks Professor!" He breathlessly moaned as he sat up right. "How do you know I am a professor?" I asked. "We were in your class today." He replied. I was not sure how I did not notice any of them, but I must have been in shock of seeing Arnold and I was not focusing on other student faces. The shock showed on my face "Do not worry, professor. What happens here, stays here" Ethan said

"Come on let's go to bed." Arnold said so I got up and went to bed with him. In his bed Arnold and I kissed and hugged for a while before we fell asleep.

9.

The following morning, I was the first to wake up and as usual I had a morning glory hard on. I stuck my hand under the sheet and gave my hard cock a couple of slow leisurely strokes. I then looked over at the hunky man beside me. The sheet was down around our stomachs so I could admire Arnold's golden tanned hunky upper body. First, I took in the sight of his handsome face, which looked serene as he slept. Next my gaze travelled down to his well-defined toned shapely pecs, which were covered in brown hairs. His nipples were big, dark brown and very chewable. I also enjoyed the vision of his tanned muscular arms which had smooth biceps but hairy forearms.

My gaze then carried on down and I saw that his cock was also hard and tenting out the bed sheet. I could clearly see the outline of his thick manly meat. I lifted the sheet off us as gentle as I could so as not to disturb him. As I did so I exposed his cock. My gaze was drawn to it at once. I saw his dense patch of brown pubes and his big hairy lightly tanned balls. I also saw his tanned muscular hairy thighs, but my attention soon turned solely to his cock. His cock was as lightly tanned as the rest of him. It was nice and thick with some prominent veins running down it. He was uncut but when he was hard his foreskin pulled all the way back, making him almost look cut. He had a swollen reddish-purple knob that was very suckable and plugged the back of my throat nicely.

I admired his body for a few minutes but my gaze always returned to his cock. I was hoping that Arnold would wake up naturally and we could have some fun together but I was horny as fuck. I also knew that he had to go into work for a couple of hours this morning as they had lost some days due to severe weather. Also, the sight of his cock hard and erect on his lightly haired tanned washboard stomach became too irresistible.

I remembered what I found out last night, that Arnold was my student. A professor having a relationship with a student is extremely against the university rules. I knew that I was putting my scholarship at risk by having sex with students. However, I was not able to battle the temptation of this man. I moved down the bed so that my head was hovering above his firm flat stomach with my mouth right near his cock. I very gently lifted his cock up between the thumb and forefinger of my left hand. I then moved my head forward and opened my mouth. As I did so I took just his knob into my mouth. I then tightly clamped my lips around his thick shaft just below the ridge of his knob. I now had his swollen sensitive knob in my mouth and I began to suck it and swarm my tongue all over it.

As soon as I started sucking on Arnold's knob and flicking it with my tongue he began to stir and moan. Gradually he came around as I continued working on his knob, which was already drooling pre-cum onto my tongue. "Nice wake up call." He moaned as he reached full consciousness. I just responded by relaxing my jaw and throat and thrust my hot wet mouth all the way down onto his manly cock until I had my nose buried in his dense patch of blond brown pubes, with his swollen knob plugging the back of my throat. I flexed my throat muscles on his swollen knob as I flicked the base of his cock with my tongue.

When the urge to breathe kicked in I pulled my mouth up his thick throbbing cock, flicking the underside with my tongue as I did so. When I reached his knob I strongly sucked it and swarmed my tongue all over, paying particular attention to the sensitive underside where his foreskin joined. As I now had his cock in my mouth my left hand was free so I started fondling his big hairy balls and caressing his muscular hairy thighs.

I then broke into a nice steady deep throating cock sucking rhythm. I bobbed my hot wet sucking mouth up and down the full length of Arnold's thick 7-inch cock. I'd work my mouth all the way down until his knob plugs the back of my throat. I'd then pull up until I just had his swollen knob in my mouth. As I did so I wanked his cock with my tightly clamped lips, caressed it with my tongue and greedily sucked on it. Arnold was moaning and groaning with pleasure as he had an avid cock sucking teen working on his manly cock. I was determined to show Arnold the full extent of my cock sucking abilities.

It felt so good having the thick cock of a sexy hunky older man in my mouth. I savoured the strong taste of his pre-cum and drank in his strong heady manly aroused aroma. I felt his hot hard thick throbbing cock sliding over my lips and tongue with his penis repeatedly plugging the back of my throat, where I'd work my throat muscles on it. I was glad I could sexually please him and from his moans and groans of pleasure I seemed to be doing a good job.

Arnold let me suck on his dick for a good 10 minutes before he suddenly surprised me by pushing me off his cock. He then flipped me onto my back before reaching into his bedside draw and fishing out a tube of lube. I watched as he greased up his lightly tanned thick manly cock, my ass practically quivering in anticipation. When he had his cock lubed up his lifted my legs and pushed them up as he got into a push up position above me. My ankles rested on his shoulders as he got into position. Steadying himself with his left hand he used his right hand to aim his cock at my ass.

I felt him rub his tool up and down my ass crack until he found my asshole. He then started applying pressure and my ass ring briefly held out. Then with a gasp from both of us my sphincter gave way and my ass lips slid down his swollen knob, over its ridge and tightly clamped around his thick throbbing shaft. Arnold didn't wait. As soon as his knob was inside my steamy tight teen boy cunt he powerfully rammed the rest of his thick throbbing meaty cock ball deep into my ass. I grunted with the rough power of the penetration, whereas Arnold gasped from the pleasure of roughly impaling my hot wet tight ass onto his thick manly cock. When he bottomed out in my ass his densely pubed groin slapped up against my pert pale ass. He held his cock ball deep in me and grounded his groin against my ass, jerking his cock about inside me.

He held his dick in my ass briefly before he started pulling it out. I felt my ass sucking and closing up after his retreating cock, which also pulled out my ass lips. He pulled his cock back until the thick ridge of his swollen knob touched the inside of my ass ring. He then slammed it back into me with a long deep hard powerful thrust making me moan at being penetrated so roughly. I felt his swollen knob force open my ass walls and bump against my prostate. His thick cock stretched and rubbed my ass lips as he rammed his cock deep into me. His densely pubed groin then slapped up against my ass, his pubes tickling my hole as his cock throbbed and twitched inside me.

Arnold then broke into a very fast rough hard passionate powerful fucking frenzy. He was using all of his hunky strength to pound my pussy boy ass. His thick meaty cock was a blur as he slammed it in and out of my ass, fucking it into submission. I was grunting and groaning at the rough fucking I was taking and although at times it was slightly painful there was far more pleasure than pain. My ass was born to be rough fucked and Arnold sure knew how to give it what it wanted.

As Arnold fucked me I looked up to watch the expressions of pleasure and exertion play across his handsome face. I admired the sight of his tensed bulging arm, chest, and shoulder muscles. With my hands I caressed and groped his hairy chest, running my fingers through his chest hairs, groping his pecs or pinching and tugging his nipples. We were both loudly moaning and groaning in pleasure as Arnold fucked me senseless and the bed was creaking under the onslaught. Beads of sweat started breaking out on us, brought on by our passionate fucking.

As we were fucking we started to hear moans and groans of pleasure and bed squeaks coming from Ronald and Ethan's room so we had obviously given them an idea. It seemed that Ronald was giving Ethan as good a seeing to as Arnold was giving me. The fact that two guys were fucking next door as Arnold fucked me made me even hornier, it just added to the situation.

By now Arnold was really slamming my ass, which was throbbing and tender but in a good way. My ass lips were also sensitive and glowing from the repeated rubbing of his thick cock stretching and stimulating them. My ass walls were throbbing from being repeatedly forced open by his swollen knob, which also hit my prostate making my cock drool pre-cum onto my stomach.

Arnold fucked me rough and hard for a good 20 minutes before he launched into a fucking frenzy. If I thought he'd been fucking me fast and hard before it was nothing compared to how he was fucking me now. I was seeing stars from having my ass fucked so rough, hard, and passionately. I was loudly grunting and groaning each time he slammed his thick meaty 7-inch cock ball deep into my tight ass, which I was flexing on his thrusting cock. His cock was a blur as he slammed it in and out, rubbing the throbbing walls of my tender young ass. The thick shaft of his cock was stretching and stimulating my sensitive ass ring making it glow with the friction. The repeated strikes of his knob against my prostate had the cum boiling in my balls and the pre-cum drooling onto my stomach.

I could tell he was getting close to orgasm so I started flexing my ass muscles on his pounding cock faster and harder. I also started roughly pinching and tugging on his dark brown nipples, which were already swollen and puffy from my earlier roughing up of them. "Yeah fuck me." I gasped. "I want to feel you cum in my ass." Arnold just grunted as he continued his rough relentless fucking of my tender battered ass.

His tempo picked up a little bit more before I felt him bang his penis into my hole. He arched his back and his face scrunched up as I felt his cock swell throb and pulse in my ass. He bucked and shuddered against me as I felt jet after jet of hot man spunk fire deep into my ass. I murmured with pleasure as I felt my boy cunt filling with cum. I wildly flexed my ass muscles on his thick orgasming cock to fuel the intensity of his orgasm and milk him dry. Arnold moaned and groaned as wave after wave of sexual pleasure flowed through his hunky body as he drained his balls into my ass.

It felt like Arnold had a massive orgasm as my ass felt full of hot cum. When he shot the last of it into me he held his cock in my ass briefly and I gently worked my ass muscles on it. He then pulled it from my tender ass and he rolled over onto his back, breathing heavily. "What a wakeup call. I sure needed that. Thanks Professor." He breathlessly said. "Tell me about it. That was some stoking you gave me." I said my ass still throbbing and my sphincter still stinging from the fucking but in a good way. I could also feel all his cum up my ass.

We lay like that for a minute or so before Arnold's bedside alarm started to go off. "Sorry, I've got to get ready for work. You'll have to take care of yourself." He said indicating down to my hard cock. "Are you going to stick around or you want me to drop you off at university?" He added. "I can't be seen with you at all, I will lose my scholarship if anyone finds out. I'll stick around if you don't mind." "Cool." Ethan will be about so if you need anything just ask him." Arnold said as he got up and headed to the bathroom naked.

When he came back I saw Ronald walk past the bedroom door on his way to the bathroom. He was naked too and I could see his big thick cock, which was rock hard, swinging about. I carried on lying on the bed as I watched Arnold get dressed. It was nice watching the muscles in his body flex as he got dressed. When he finished dressing he asked,

"Do you want any breakfast?" "No thanks. I think I'll go back to sleep." "Lucky bugger." "You did the buggering." I jokingly replied which made him chuckle too. With that he went down to have breakfast. I then pulled up the sheet and went to sleep. Even though I had a raging hard on and had been so turned on and horny from the fucking Arnold had given I didn't want to waste my cum on a wank and instead decided to wait for Arnold to return.

10.

I managed to grab some more sleep before I woke up again. I still had a hard on but this time it was more of a piss hard on. I got up and headed towards the bathroom, my hard erect 6.5-inch cock pointing the way. I went into the bathroom and had a piss. I then hoped in the shower and got cleaned up. I then went back to Arnold's room and dug out a pair of his shorts. They were a bit big and baggy but I hadn't heard Ethan get up yet so I didn't want to wake him. I then went downstairs to get something to eat and watch TV until Arnold returned.

As I walked past Ronald and Ethan's room I saw that the door was fully open. I knew Ethan was home because he was a plasterer whereas Arnold and Ronald were brickies. Ethan couldn't do anything on the site until the brickies got back on track. As I walked past I just couldn't help but look in. What I saw stopped me short. I saw Ethan on the bed stark naked. What was more he was slowly wanking his hard cock with his right hand. I couldn't help but admire his very sexy lightly tanned face with its look of pleasure. My gaze then quickly took in his subtly toned, lightly tanned chest, arms, and flat firm stomach. My gaze then dropped to his lightly tanned 7-inch uncut cock, watching his foreskin peeling back and forth over his swollen pinky red knob as he slowly wanked it. His tanned hairy balls were rising and falling as he stroked his cock. My gaze then ran down his muscular tanned hairy thighs before returning back to his cock. I did all this in a flash, taking a mental photo of the scene before me.

I was about to carry on my way when Ethan asked, "Want to give me a hand?" "Will Ronald be OK with it?" I asked, not wanting to become between them. "He was OK with it last night." Ethan added, a wonderfully sexy smile spreading across his face. I was not sure where my relationship with Arnold was and he was ok with it the night before. My sexual drive was stronger than ever and there was no way I will be able to stop myself even the risk of losing my scholarship.

I went into the room and got onto the bed beside Ethan. I looked into his sexy lightly tanned face and dreamy brown eyes as I started to caress his subtly toned chest, which had a dusting of blond brown peach fuzz. I liked feeling his soft hairs under my fingers as I started circling them around his small left brown nipple. Goose bumps soon came up around it and the nub started to stiffen and swell. I then began to gently pinch and rub it between my thumb and forefinger.

After a bit I moved my hand over to his right nipple and began gently pinching and rubbing that as I leant forward and started circling my tongue around his left nipple. I circled around it and licked my tongue over it before gently gripping it between my teeth where I gently chewed and tugged it. As I did this I could see his sexy tanned uncut cock wildly throbbing on his flat firm stomach. He'd stopped wanking it now and had let it fall from his grip.

I licked, chewed, and pinched his nipples for a couple of minutes before his tanned throbbing cock lured me away. I began kissing, licking, and caressing my way down his tanned flat firm stomach, which had a dusting of peach fuzz on it. When I reached the tip of his cock I firmly gripped it in my left hand and peeled back the foreskin. I felt its thick warm throbbing pulse in my hand as I stuck my tongue out and licked up his pearl of pre-cum. I savoured its taste before I started swarming my tongue all over his pinky red swollen knob. Ethan began to purr with pleasure as I licked all over his sensitive knob. As I licked his knob I felt his cock throb harder in my hand.

Ethan ran his fingers through my shaggy hair as I licked his knob like a favourite lollipop. From his moans of pleasure and the amount of pre-cum he was drooling onto my tongue he seemed to be enjoying it. I then kissed the tip of his cock and relaxed my jaw and throat and started to push my mouth onto his dick. My lips parted and slid down over his knob and its thick ridge before tightly clamping around his throbbing shaft. I briefly sucked and licked his knob before I carried on forcing my mouth down onto his cock. Inch by inch I took more and more of it into my mouth. Soon I had my nose buried in his dense patch of blond brown pubes with his knob plugging the back of my throat. I flexed my throat muscles on his knob as I felt his 7-inch cock throb and pulse in my mouth as I flicked the base with my tongue. I drank in his sweaty manly aroused aroma before I pulled my mouth back up his cock, wanking it with my lips, caressing it with my tongue and sucking it until I just had his swollen sensitive knob in my mouth.

I then broke into a nice steady cock sucking rhythm, bobbing my mouth on Ethan's sexy hot hard cock like a yoyo. To start with I kept deep throating him, taking all 7 inches into my mouth. Then I started alternating my style. One moment I was deep throating him and the next I was just sucking and licking his swollen sensitive knob. I also licked up and down his cock like a lollipop or bobbed my mouth half way up and down his cock. From his moans of pleasure and the way his cock was throbbing I could tell I was doing a good job.

I sucked on his cock for quite a while, really getting into it. I was really enjoying his sweaty aroused smell, the taste of his pre-cum and the feel of his sexy throbbing cock in my mouth. However, despite enjoying sucking on his cock so much my ass started itching for another fucking. I pulled my mouth off his cock and straddled his midriff. I looked into his sexy face and deep dreamy brown eyes as I reached behind me and gripped his throbbing saliva soaked cock. I rubbed his knob up and down my ass crack until I found my hole and nestled his knob against it.

I then started forcing my ass down onto his upward pointing cock which I was gripping at the base. I felt the pressure increase on my ass lips, which soon parted and started sliding down his swollen knob. We both gasped when they slid over the thick ridge of his knob and tightly clamped around his shaft. As soon the ridge of his knob passed my ass lips I thrust my ass down hard onto his upright cock. We both grunted with pleasure as I impaled my tight cummy ass on Ethan's thick throbbing 7-inch dick. I held my ass on his cock for a bit, his densely pubed groin pressed tight against my ass as I flexed my ass muscles on his hot hard cock. As I remained sat on his cock I reached forward and started caressing his downy haired, subtly toned chest. I also took in the look of pleasure on his gorgeous face.

I then lifted my ass up his cock feeling my ass lips being pulled outwards by his thick shaft as my ass closed up after his retreating cock. I pulled up until the ridge of his knob butted up against my ass ring. Without hesitation I slammed my ass back down onto his cock, swallowing all 7 inches in one go. We both moaned with pleasure, me from thrusting my sensitive ass onto his hot hard throbbing 7-inch cock and Ethan from having me impale my hot wet tight cum filled ass on to his cock. As I thrust my ass down his joystick forced open my cummy ass walls and as it was rubbing against the front wall of my ass it hit my prostate on its way deep into me. When it did so my cock twitched and drooled some pre-cum onto his tanned stomach.

I broke into a nice steady fast rhythm, bouncing my ass up and down on Ethan's cock, taking it all the way in to the pubed hilt. Feeling his cock forcing open my ass felt so good and waves of pleasure started radiating out from my ass. I could also feel Arnold's cum bubbling around Ethan's cock as he fucked me. As I rode his joystick I looked down at his sexy face and tanned upper body before me. He had light blond hair and a stunningly sexy face, with lush pink kissable lips and dreamy brown eyes. I also saw his sexy subtly toned, golden tanned chest with dark brown nipples. I felt the firmness of his chest and the soft downiness of its hairs as I caressed and groped his pecs, occasionally pinching his nipples.

We were soon both moaning and groaning in pleasure as I rode his cock like a cowboy. I was using the strength in my thighs to power my bouncing on his cock. As I bounced my ass sucked at his cock, the hot wet cummy walls of my ass and his foreskin caressed his swollen knob as my tight ass lips wanked his thick throbbing cock. When I slammed my ass down onto his cock I felt his densely pubed groin slap against my ass, with his pubes tickling my hole. Waves of pleasure were radiating out from my stuffed ass as I thrust it up and down on his hot hard cock. The smell of gay sex also filled the room and added to the horniness. My hands were swarming all over his sexy chest and roughing up his nipples as I watched the looks of sexual ecstasy play across his well sexy face.

I rode his hot thick throbbing 7-inch cock for ages, really getting off on the pleasure it was giving me. However due to the position we were fucking in his swollen knob rubbed the front wall of my ass and repeatedly hit my prostate. This just added and intensified the pleasurable feeling of his cock slamming my ass, his sexy good looks, and the excitement of fucking behind our partner's backs. It also had the cum boiling in my balls especially since Arnold almost made me cum when he fucked me earlier. Taking my second fucking of the day proved too much and I felt the pressure in my balls reach critical mass.

I managed to bounce my ass up and down his rock-hard meat a few more times, his knob hitting my prostate each time. I slammed my ass down again and his knob hit my prostate which was the trigger. I arched my back and loudly cried out as cum exploded from my cock. The first jet was so powerful it arched through the air and splashed onto Ethan's sexy face. Six more big powerful spurts of hot thick cum exploded out of my cock and splashed on his tanned chest and stomach. As I came I loudly moaned and groaned with pleasure as wave after wave of intense sexual pleasure flowed through my body. I bucked and ground my ass onto his hard cock, my ass spasming uncontrollably around it as I covered him in cum.

I couldn't believe how intense my orgasm was or how much cum I'd shot considering I'd already cum a load the night before. As I weakly shot the last of my load into Ethan's dense patch of blond brown pubes I looked down at his tanned chest and stomach which had cum splatters all over them. I also saw him stick out his tongue and lick up my cum from around his mouth. He took it into his mouth and savoured my spunk.

My orgasm had left me exhausted and I collapsed forward so that I was sat on my heels but lent forward with my hands on the bed supporting my upper body. My thighs were burning from the exertion and I was totally spent but Ethan hadn't cum and he was close. He suddenly gripped my ass and lifted it up as he thrust his ass down into the bed. He then rammed his cock upwards as he yanked my ass down onto his cock. With a loud grunt from both of us his groin slapped against my ass as he buried all 7 inches of his hot throbbing cock ball deep into my ass. He then launched into a fast-hard powerful fucking frenzy.

I went limp and let him control the fuck. He used his grip on my ass to bounce it on his cock and he thrust it up and down, making sure he got maximum penetration. My ass was on fire from the pleasure of the hard fucking it was taking. His swollen sensitive knob was forcing open and caressing the tender walls of my ass. My sphincter was glowing from being stretched and stimulated by his hot thick shaft rubbing it. My ass was being slapped by his densely pubed groin hitting it. As I came down from my post orgasm high I started flexing my ass muscles on his thrusting cock faster and harder, increasing the pleasure for both of us. As my strength returned I took my hands off the bed and started helping Ethan with bouncing my ass on his cock as I started roughly pinching and tugging his puffy nipples.

We fucked like this for a couple more minutes grunting and groaning like two rutting stags as my tight ass bounced up and down his cock like a yoyo. "Going to cum." Ethan gasped and I saw his sexy face scrunch up. Then he yanked my ass down as he powerfully thrust his cock upwards. His densely pubed groin loudly and firmly slapped up against my ass, his rigid knob ramming open my ass walls as he buried it ball deep into my cummy ass. I felt his cock swell and pulse as he started bucking against me and blasting jet after jet of hot cum into my ass, adding to the load that Arnold had already fired up there earlier. Ethan moaned and groaned as he spunked a big load of hot cum up my very tender, satisfied, well fucked ass, looks of sexual ecstasy playing across his gorgeous face. I purred with pleasure as I felt him fire his cum into me and I flexed my ass muscles on his orgasming cock to fuel his orgasm and milk him dry.

When he finished cumming he collapsed onto the bed, lost in the post orgasm glow. I slowly pulled my tender cum filled ass off his rod. I then lay beside him to rest my legs. I saw the trails of my cum on his tanned chest. I just couldn't help but start to lick my thick cooling cum form his body. I savoured the taste of my own jizz as I worked my way down his body. As I licked up the last of it I saw Ethan's still hard spent cock which was glistening with a combination of Arnold's cum, Ethan's cum and my ass juice. As there was no shit I just gripped his cock and stuck my mouth onto it. I took about half of it into my mouth and tightly clamped my lips around his thick shaft and began to suck it. Immediately the taste of cum and ass juice hit my tongue and it was delicious. I started bobbing my mouth up and down his cock sucking it clean.

When it was clean I let it fall from my mouth and I lay on my side to Ethan's left and admired his sexy body as we recovered from our fuck. When we got our breath back Ethan went for shower while I stayed laid on the bed. When he came back I asked him if I could borrow some of his shorts as Arnold's were a bit big. He went to his draw and threw me a pair of white footie shorts that must have been too small for him as they were a snug fit on me and I was only a slim lean teen. We then went downstairs and had breakfast before watching TV waiting for our partners to return.

11.

A couple of hours later Arnold & Ronald returned and found Ethan and I sat just in shorts side by side watching TV. "You reckon they've been up to no good while we've been at work?" Ronald asked Arnold as he sat down on a sofa. "Considering they're both tarts I think it's a cert." Arnold light heartedly replied. "He threw himself at me." Ethan jokingly added. "I don't doubt that." Arnold said as he sat next to Ronald.

We watched some TV before Ronald chipped in and asked Arnold "Do you fancy swapping bitches? I'd love to nail the professor." "Fine by me." Arnold replied. I was a bit surprised at being pimped out like this. I thought that Arnold would want sex with me but instead he'd offered me to one of his flat mates, while he wanted to fuck the other one. Almost as soon as Arnold had given Ronald the green light he unzipped his dusty work jeans and pulled out his cock which was already hard and erect.

I looked over in awe at Ronald's hard cock. It was the biggest I'd seen so far. My earlier biggest had been Leroy, who had a nice thick 8-inch black cock. Ronald's was a little bit thicker and 8.5 inches long. Unlike Leroy's cock Ronald's was cut so all of his large swollen knob was exposed. It sure looked like a mouth and ass stretcher. "Come and wrap those hot lips around my cock." Ronald said as he waved it at me. I looked to Arnold and he gave me the go-ahead nod. I got of the sofa and walked over to where they were sat. I knelt on the floor and admired his impressive chopper up close as I hooked my fingers under the waistband of his jeans and boxers. I started to tug them down was Ronald lifted his ass off the sofa.

I continued to stare at his big thick throbbing cock as I pulled his jeans down and then off. I briefly admired his pale firm toned legs, which were finely covered in dark brown hairs. However, my gaze was always brought back to his hot cock. His cock was pale like the rest of him. It was quite veiny, very thick, 8.5 inches long and neatly cut with a large swollen pinky purple knob. I was fascinated by his cut knob as most guys in the UK are uncut. Ronald's was only the second circumcised cock I'd seen. Now while I preferred uncut cock there was something to be said about the novelty of a cut cock. I also took in the sight of his big pale tight balls.

After admiring his cock, I leant forward and gave his balls a long lick. I tasted and smelt his sweaty aroused aroma and I found it very erotic. I then started licking away at his balls as I caressed his firm toned thighs. As I was doing this Arnold pushed down his jeans and Ethan came and knelt beside me, in between Arnold's muscular tanned hairy legs. Ethan took a leaf out of my book and licked away at Arnold's balls like I was doing to his boyfriend's balls.

I licked Ronald's sweaty balls before licking one into my mouth and gently sucking it. I then did the same to his other ball. However, his big thick throbbing dick soon became too irresistible to my hungry mouth. I dragged my hot wet tongue up the underside of his thick meaty veiny cock from the base up to his large swollen cut knob. I licked up the drop of tasty pre-cum before I started flicking my tongue over the sensitive underside of his knob where his foreskin would have joined. Ronald moaned with pleasure as I licked the underside of his knob.

As I licked the underside of his cut knob he started oozing pre-cum which dribbled down his knob and onto my tongue. I savoured it strong taste as I drank in his sweaty manly aroused aroma. I then started swarming my tongue all over his large swollen cut knob, which made Ronald moan even more with pleasure. Beside me Ethan was also swarming his tongue all over my partner's knob.

Ronald pulled his tee shirt tee shirt off as I licked his knob like a favourite lollipop. I admired his pale toned upper body with its small patch of dark hairs between his pecs. His nipples were small, pink, and pointy and looked very chewable. Ronald began to caress his own upper body and rub his nipples until they became hard and erect. He then turned to Arnold and they began to passionately kiss each other as Ethan and I worked on their cocks. They also began to caress each other's toned upper bodies and pinch each other's nipples.

Seeing Ronald and Arnold snogging away as I licked Ronald's knob was a real turn on. However, the urge to test my cock sucking abilities on Ronald's big cock soon overrode that. I kissed the tip of Ronald's cock and then started forcing my mouth down onto his cock. My lips parted and started sliding down over his large swollen knob. They slipped down over the thick ridge of his knob which stretched them wide. When they past his ridge I clamped them around his thick meaty shaft. His rod was almost as thick as the ridge of his knob so they will still stretch wide. With just his large swollen knob in my mouth I began to greedily suck it as I swarmed my tongue all over it. This made him drool even more tasty pre-cum into my mouth which I savoured.

I sucked on Ronald's knob for a few minutes as Ethan did the same to Arnold's. I then relaxed my jaw and throat and started pushing my mouth down onto his big thick cock. His cock was so thick I was only able to take half of it in before my lips and jaw were stretched to the max. There was still plenty of room at the back of my throat for his big cock but he was too thick to take any more in. Instead I started sucking and flicking my tongue on the part of his cock as I could take. I then started bobbing my mouth up and down his cock, sliding my tightly clamped lips and hot sucking mouth up and down his cock, caressing it with my tongue as I did so.

I spent a good few minutes working on Ronald's manhood as he snogged Arnold. Because his cock was so thick I had to alternate between bobbing my hot wet sucking mouth up and down it and licking it like a lollipop or rubbing my pursed on it. Either way he seemed to be enjoying it from the way his cock was wildly throbbing and the amount of pre-cum he was drooling. Occasionally I glanced to my right and watched Ethan sucking on my partner's cock. It was so hot watching his gorgeous tanned face bobbing up and down on Arnold tanned manly cock.

Ronald let me suck away on his tool for a while before he wanted something else. This was perfect timing as my mouth and jaw was really beginning to ache from sucking his thick cock. Ronald broke off his kiss with Arnold and looked down at me. "Thanks Professor, that was good but I want to feel your tight young ass on my big cock." He said as he lifted my head up so that I was looking at him. I noticed he had a very lusty look on his slightly rough, mean but sexy face. "I need to fuck too." Arnold added as he pulled his cock from Ethan's mouth. "Sit on the sofa over there." Ronald instructed and Ethan and I obeyed.

Ethan and I sat side by side on one of the other sofas. Ronald and Arnold got up and walked over to us, their hard-thick manly cocks pointing the way. As they walked towards us I couldn't help but admired their fit sexy bodies. First, I took in the sight of Ronald's body as I wasn't as familiar with it as I was with Arnold's.

Ronald wasn't as muscular as Arnold but he still had a well-defined body and was more toned than Ethan. His face had a kind of mean street look about it but it was still sexy. His hair was dark brown and he had grey eyes. He was pale all over with nicely toned arms with smooth biceps and lightly haired forearms. His chest was toned and pale with pink nipples and a small patch of soft dark chest hairs between them. His stomach was pale and flat with a small trimmed patch of dark brown pubes. He had nice big tight balls and his impressive thick meaty 8.5 inch cut cock pointed downwards under its own meaty weight. He had sexy pale toned legs that were covered in dark brown hairs.

After admiring Ronald's fit sexy body, I briefly turned my attention to Arnold. I admired his tanned handsome face and blue eyes, which were framed by his centre parted dark blond hair. I observed at his well-toned hunky tanned chest which was densely covered in dark blond chest hairs. His tanned washboard stomach was also covered in dark blond hairs leading down into a dense patch of blond brown pubes. His cock was as tanned as the rest of him, 7 inches long, uncut and a nice thickness. He had nice big tanned low hanging balls and very sexy muscular tanned hairy legs.

Ronald then stood in front of me while Arnold walked past us to get some lube out of the sideboard draw. With his impressive cock inches from my face I just couldn't resist taking it back into my mouth. I wrapped my lips tightly around his thick throbbing shaft about two inches down it. I then started strongly sucking on his cock as I swarmed my tongue all over his knob. "He sure knows how to suck cock." Ronald moaned. Almost in unison Arnold and Ethan agreed. This made me swell with pride that three fit sexy older guys thought that even though I was only 18 I was a good cock sucker.

Arnold soon returned with the lube and passed it to Ronald first. He pulled his cock from my mouth and I watched in awe as he started lubing up his thick meaty cock. His right hand slid up and down his cock, greasing up all 8.5 inches of it. He then squirted some lube onto his hand before passing the tube to Arnold. "Lift up your legs." Ronald instructed as Arnold started lubing up his cock. I lifted my legs up and pulled them into my chest, grabbing them behind my knees to hold them in place. Ronald then started rubbing the cool lube onto my asshole before he finger fucked some of it up my ass.

To start with he just used one finger but as my ass relaxed he added more until he was thrusting all four fingers in and out of my ass making sure it was ready to take his big thick meaty manhood. By now Arnold had finished lubing up his cock and was starting to rub some lube onto Ethan's ass. Ronald then got into position above me. I rested my ankles on his shoulders as he supported his weight with his hands on the edge of the sofa and the balls of his feet on the floor. As his hands were occupied I gripped his thick cock in my left hand. I felt its thick meaty girth and warm throbbing pulse. As I felt how thick it was in my hand I began to doubt whether my tight ass would be able to take it. However, my cock hungry pussy boy nature came to the fore and I rubbed his knob up and down my ass crack until I found my asshole.

When I found the entrance to my ass I held Ronald's large swollen cut knob against it. I felt him start to apply pressure. My ass ring briefly held out as he increased the pressure. Then with a sharp searing stinging pain, which cause me to yelp out, his large knob forced open my ass ring. My ass lips slid down over his flared cut knob and over its thick ridge before snapping shut around his thick meaty cock. My ass lips felt stretched to the max and I was panting as I tried to overcome the initial pain of being penetrated by such a thick meaty cock. Ronald held just his knob inside my ass to give me time to get used to it.

When he felt my ass relax he slowly started forcing the rest of his big cock into me. Inch by inch more of it entered my ass forcing open my love chute wider than it had ever been before. Beside me Arnold had got into position above Ethan and had thrust his 7-inch cock into Ethan's ass in one go. However, Arnold's cock wasn't as long or as thick as Ronald's and this was the first time I'd taken his penis.

Soon Ronald bottomed out in my ass with his pubed groin pressed against my ass. My ass had never felt so full and stretched by cock. It was so stuffed of cock that it was mildly uncomfortable. His swollen knob was probing parts of my ass no cock had touched before. His thick meaty shaft had my ass lips so stretched they were mildly stinging. I felt the heat and throbbing pulse of his cock as he held it inside me. He held it there so that I could get used to having such a big thick meaty cock in my ass. I panted as I slowly recovered. I then started flexing my ass muscles on it which seemed to lessen the pain.

Ronald took my ass flexing as a sign that I was now ready to be fucked. He slowly pulled his cock backwards and I felt it pulling my ass lips outwards as my ass closed behind his retreating cock. He pulled back until the thick ridge of his penis butted up against the inside of my pucker. He then thrust it back into my ass ball deep. Although he did it slowly it was a little faster than the first thrust. I gasped as I felt his large swollen knob forcing open my ass walls as his thick shaft stretched and rubbed ass lips. On its way deep into my hot wet steamy tight ass, his knob bumped against my prostate which made my cock twitch on my stomach and drool some pre-cum.

Ronald held his big meat inside me briefly, jerking it about before he pulled back. He then broke into a slow steady fucking rhythm. He was letting me get used to taking his big thick cock but I knew there was pure lust and passion bubbling under the surface just waiting to break out and fuck me senseless. My well stretched ass felt every thrust of his cock. His large swollen knob forced open and rubbed my ass walls, hitting my prostate. His thick shaft stretched and stimulated my ass ring to the max, which was tickled by his pubes when he bottomed out in me. I looked up at his pale tensed upper body and the looks of pleasure on his sexy face as he slid his big thick cock in and out of my hot wet tight ass. Never had my ass felt so full of cock. It was uncomfortable but with each thrust that began to fade and be replaced by pleasure.

As Ronald picked up the pace my ass began to feel it even more but it was more pleasure now than anything. As he fucked me I alternated my gaze from admiring his sexy face and toned body to look over to my left and watch Arnold fucking Ethan. As Ethan was used to taking Ronald's and Arnold's cock Arnold didn't need to be as gentle with Ethan as Ronald needed to be with me. Instead Arnold was slamming his tanned thick 7-inch manhood in and out of Ethan's tanned ass like a jack hammer. Ethan was loudly moaning and groaning with pleasure as he took my partner's cock. It sure was a hot sight watching hunky Arnold fucking sexy Ethan.

My ass adapted quickly to Ronald's big thick cock, which meant that he could now fuck me faster and harder. He picked up his fucking pace, his large swollen cut knob forcing open my ass walls as he slammed his cock ball deep into me. My ass lips were well stretched and having his thick cock rubbing them made them glow with pleasurable friction. Once I'd recovered from the initial discomfort and mild pain of having such a big thick cock fucking my ass I began to really get into it. The pain faded and was replaced with a well stuffed pleasure. I could feel Ronald's cock stretching and penetrating my tight ass to the max, testing its cock taking abilities. I also started flexing my ass muscles on his cock, gripping it tight when the thrust his cock in and relaxing when he pulled out. I felt his thick shaft rubbing my ass lips and pulling them outward when he pulled his cock back. His large swollen thick ridged knob forced open and caress my ass walls, hitting my prostate on each thrust. I also began to lustily moan and tell Ronald how good it felt having his big cock fucking my ass.

Ronald quickly picked up his pace so that he was soon fucking me as hard rough and passionately as Arnold was fucking Ethan. Like me Ethan was deliriously moaning with sexual pleasure as my partner fucked him. I watched fascinated as Arnold's tanned thick cock slid in and out of Ethan's tanned ass. I also saw Ethan's sexy tanned uncut cock throbbing on his stomach. It looked so sexy I knew I just had to take it into my mouth. As Ronald continued pounding my ass I leant over and gripped Ethan's cock in my right hand. I felt its warm throbbing pulse as I gave it a few wanks, peeling his foreskin back and forth over his pinky red knob. I then opened my mouth and took just the knob into my mouth and tightly clamped my lips around his shaft just below the ridge of his knob.

With Ethan's knob in my mouth I began to greedily suck it and swarm my tongue all over it. This made him moan even more as he had pleasure flowing down his cock from my mouth and radiating out from his ass from having Arnold fuck him. I savoured the pleasure of taking cock at both ends. I felt Ethan's smooth hot hard rod sliding over my lips and tongue as it drooled loads of tasty pre-cum onto my tongue. I also drank in his musky sweaty manly aroused aroma and the smell of gay sex. Sucking Ethan's cock also gave me an up-close bird's eye view of Arnold's thick tanned manly cock slamming in and out of Ethan's ass. Arnold really was giving Ethan a dam good seeing too.

At the other end my ass was throbbing and glowing from the pleasure of being fucked rough hard and fast by the biggest cock I had taken in my life up to the point. Never had my tight ass felt so full, stretched, or penetrated by cock. His large swollen cut knob was stimulating parts of my young slutty ass that no cock had reached before. My ass lips were stretched to the max and glowing with the pleasurable friction of taking such a thick cock. I felt his cock's heat and throbbing pulse as he powerfully banged my ass like a jack hammer. He was really making sure my ass felt the fuck. Each time he slammed his cock into me his knob hit my prostate which made the cum boil in my balls.

We fucked like this for ages. Ronald was fucking my ass as I sucked off Ethan's cock, while Arnold fucked Ethan's ass. Both Ronald and Arnold were fucking Ethan and I like mad. All four of us were loudly grunting with sexual pleasure. My ass had become hyper sensitive, but in a good way, from the rough hard fucking Ronald was giving it with his big thick cock. I knew that Arnold and Ronald must be getting close as they both slipped into a passionate fucking frenzy, using all the strength to slam their cocks into our willing asses. I could see Arnold's cock was a blur as it pounded in and out of Ethan's ass, his densely pubed groin slapping against Ethan's tanned ass.

It was Arnold who came first. He was really slamming his dick in and out of Ethan's ass when he moaned he was going to cum. He gave Ethan's ass another few deep hard powerful thrusts before he slammed it ball deep into his ass one last time. He then started bucking and shuddering against Ethan, loudly crying out in pleasure as he started pumping jet after jet of hot cum deep inside Ethan's ass. Ethan started purring with pleasure as he felt his ass filling up with cum.

Ethan came second. Having Arnold fuck his ass long, rough, and hard and then fill it with cum as he had a horny teen sucking on his cock sent him over the edge. Arnold's orgasm had just finished and he was gently grinding his spent but still rock-hard cock in Ethan's cum filled ass. I was just sucking on Ethan's swollen knob and swarming my tongue all over it when I felt his body tense up. I then felt his cock swell throb and pulse in my hand and mouth as it started blasting jet after jet of hot thick tasty cum into my mouth. I felt 6 big squirts of cum fire into my mouth and I let it all pool there so I could savour its taste.

When Ethan's stopped cumming I pulled my mouth off his cock and swirled his delicious cum around my mouth before I greedily swallowed it. I then went back to gently sucking on his knob before it became too sensitive for him. However, my mouth wasn't empty for long as Arnold pulled his spent hard cock out of Ethan's ass. I could see it was glistening with Arnold's cum and Ethan's ass juice. Before I knew what, I was doing I had Arnold's cock in my mouth and I was sucking it clean, tasting the saltiness of Arnold's cum and the funkiness of Ethan's ass.

At was at this point that Ronald slammed his cock into my ass hard and his large swollen knob bumped my prostate. That was the final trigger for me. My ass was throbbing and sensitive but in a good way from being fucked so long and hard by such a big thick cock. There had also been the pleasure of sucking off Ethan's tanned sexy cock and getting a mouthful of tasty spunk. I was still sucking on Arnold's cock when I started blasting jet after jet of hot teen spunk all over my chest and stomach.

I couldn't believe how powerful and intense my orgasm had been. I pumped 6 big jets of cum, which splattered on my smooth flat chest and stomach. As I came my ass muscles spasmed uncontrollably around Ronald's massive cock, which sent him into a fucking frenzy. I was seeing stars he was fucking me so fast and hard with his hot thick 8.5-inch cock. My orgasm made my ass even more sensitive and receptive to the fucking Ronald was giving it, which in turn fuelled the intensity of my orgasm.

When I finished spunking up Ethan leaned over and started licking my teen spunk off my body. It was while he was doing this that Ronald came. I was loudly grunting from having such a big thick penis slammed up my tight ass so fast hard and powerfully. It really was on the pleasure pain barrier with my ass lips glowing and my ass walls throbbing. I felt him smash his hot cock deep into my ass, his pubed groin firmly slapping up against my pert ass. I felt his cock swell throb and pulse as it started blasting hot cum deep into my teen boy ass. Ronald loudly cried out with pleasure and I moaned with delight as I felt his hot man spunk filling my very tender, sensitive, throbbing battered but very satisfied ass. Ronald bucked and shuddered against me as he drained his balls into my ass. I felt every blast coat my ass walls and relished the sensation.

When Ronald finished cumming he slowly pulled his big cock from my sensitive ass. As soon as it was out Ethan took it into his mouth and sucked it clean of his boyfriend's cum and my ass juice. I sat there in sexual heaven still coming down from the sexual high of my orgasm and from the rough hard passionate fucking from such a thick meaty big cock. My ass had been fucked three times today and it was certainly feeling it. Never before had it felt so stretched, tender or sensitive. Despite that it also felt dam good and had sure been worth it. Already I was missing Ronald's cock and I could feel the cum up it.

After we recovered I got dressed and went home as I had a lot of studying and preparation to do for my next class. I snogged Arnold for a few minutes before I left. As soon as I got out of their house, I started to feel all the cum leaking out from my tender sensitive well fucked ass, and it felt amazing. I knew that I would will be back.

12.

At the weekend I arranged to meet Arnold just
down the road from university where he'd pick me
up so no one would see us together. As planned I
met up with Arnold but was surprised to see that
Ronald and Ethan were with him. Ethan was in the
back of the van and I jumped in with him. Arnold
was driving with Ronald sat in the passenger seat.
The back of the van was full of tools and a big long
metal tool chest. It was this that Ethan and I sat
on as Arnold drove us out to the countryside.
When he found a suitably secluded spot he pulled
over into a lay by.

Almost as soon as I got into the back of the van
with Ethan, we started getting it on together. He
was wearing a dusty dark blue tee shirt, beige
shorts, thick walking socks and work boots. I just
had time to say hi to the three of them and admire
Ethan before we started passionately snogging
away. I took in the sight of his truly gorgeous
tanned, handsome face with its dusting of freckles
and dreamy brown eyes. I also got a quick look at
his tanned, lightly haired forearms and very sexy,
tanned, toned, hairy legs. As we kissed each other,
our lips locked and tongues fencing, we began to
strip each other off, even though we were still
driving. Ethan went first by pulling off my tee shirt.
I quickly followed suit but I held his arms up, the
sleeves of his tee shirt acting as a shackle around
his elbows. This meant that his sweaty hairy pits
were on show. I immediately dove in and began
eagerly licking out his left armpit. I drank in its

sweaty manly smell and lapped up the salty sweat. Ethan purred with pleasure as I gave his pit a tongue bath.

Once I'd licked it out I kissed and licked my way over his tanned, subtly toned chest to his dark brown left nipple, which had a light dusting of soft light brown hair around it. I circled my tongue around it, which made it come out in goose bumps and start to harden, the hairs tickling my tongue. As his nipple became more erect I started flicking my tongue over it. Ethan ran his fingers through my shaggy hair, purring with pleasure. Once his nipple was fully hard I started to gently suck and chew it. When it became red and puffy I licked my way over to his right nipple and gave it the same treatment.

After getting his right nipple to the same state as his left I kissed and licked my way to his right sweaty, hairy armpit which I greedily licked out. I then got up and knelt on the floor between his legs as he finished pulling off his tee shirt. We were still driving about as I began to undo his shorts, licking out his navel, which was surrounded by soft brown hairs, as I did so. Once his shorts were open I started pulling them down and he lifted his ass off the tool chest, which had foam padding on the top. As I pulled his shorts down, I exposed his hard, watched his sexy, golden tanned cock with his pinky red knob half peeking out of its foreskin. His big tanned, hairy balls nestled underneath his hot dick as I pulled his shorts further down. As I did so more and more of his very sexy, toned, shapely, tanned hairy legs came into view. My gaze travelled down them as I pulled off his shorts. My gaze then ran back up them before settling on his cock.

I admired his sexy cock for a bit longer before I firmly gripped it in my left hand. I felt its warm throbbing pulse as I slowly wanked it with a couple of firm strokes. I watched as his tanned foreskin peeled back and forth over his swollen pinky red knob. Already his sweaty manly aroma was filling my nostrils. As a plasterer he'd worked up a sweat during his morning shift and now his pheromones where adding to it. I gave his cock a few wanks before I peeled his foreskin all the way back and flicked my tongue over the sensitive underside where his foreskin joined. I heard Ethan moan with pleasure as I lapped away at the sensitive patch of skin, his hot cock wildly throbbing in my hand.

I spent a minute or so just licking the underside of his swollen knob before I started swarming my tongue all over it. I tasted its saltiness and felt the texture of it against my tongue as his sweaty, manly aroused smell filled my nose and the sight of his sexy cock and hairy groin filled my vision. I gave his swollen, sensitive knob a good licking before I kissed the tip and started forcing my mouth down onto his cock. My lips parted and started sliding down his flared knob. They slid down over the ridge of his knob before tightly clamping around his shaft below it. With just his knob in my mouth I began to greedily suck and lick away at it, feeling and tasting his pre-cum drooling onto my tongue.

As I sucked and licked away on his knob I used my hands to caress his sexy, hairy toned thighs, feeling the softness of the hairs and firmness of the muscles under my exploring hands. I then relaxed my mouth and throat and started forcing my cock hungry mouth further down onto his hot, hard, throbbing cock. Inch by inch I took more and more of his tanned 7-inch cock into my mouth until I had my nose buried in his dense patch of light brown pubes with his swollen knob plugging the back of my throat. Ethan gasped as I swallowed his rod whole and worked my throat muscles on the head. I held it ball deep in my mouth as long as I could, flicking the base as I did so before slowly pulling up until I just had the head in my mouth. I gave his knob a quick suck and lick before I forced my mouth back down onto his cock. Like before, I took all 7 throbbing inches into my mouth and flicked the base with my tongue as I worked my throat muscles on the head.

After that I broke into a slow, steady, deep throating cock sucking rhythm. I worked my hot wet mouth up and down the full length of his cock, greedily sucking it like the cock sucking teen whore I was. As I did so I wanked it with my tightly clamped lips and caressed it with my tongue. My hands were caressing his toned hairy thighs as I drank in his sweaty, horny aroused smell and listened to his moans of pleasure. As for Ethan he just leaned back and savoured the oral pleasure I was lavishing on his cock. It felt so good having his hot, hard, throbbing cock sliding in and out of my mouth, rubbing my lips and tongue. The taste of his delicious pre-cum made my tongue tingle and fuelled my cock hunger.

I was really getting into deep throating Ethan's cock when Arnold finally found a place that looked quite enough for us to pull over in. "We haven't got that long so you two better get down to it." Arnold instructed over the back of his seat. Ethan and I certainly didn't need telling twice. I stood up and the obvious tent in my trackie bottoms became eye level with Ethan. He rubbed my hard-throbbing cock through the satiny material of my trackie bottoms before he started pulling them down. As usual I wasn't wearing any underwear so my 6.5-inch cock sprang out and bounced about as he pulled my trackies down to my ankles. I kept my trainers on with my trackies around my ankles, like shackles as Ethan firmly gripped my pale, toned ass, and pulled me towards him. As he did so he opened his mouth and engulfed my cock all the way down to the pubed hilt. I gasped with pleasure as Ethan took my sensitive cock into his hot, wet mouth and gave it a few sucks.

As he bobbed his hot, wet sucking mouth up and down my throbbing cock he greased up his sexy tanned cock. Once he was suitably lubed up he stood up and we swapped positions. I laid length ways on the tool box, lifted my legs up and gripped them behind my knees. Ethan got into a squat position above me and I rested my ankles on his shoulders. He supported his weight on his left arm which made the tanned muscles in it bulge. With his right hand he gripped his cock and rubbed it up and down my ass crack as he searched out my hole. When he found it, he pressed his swollen knob against the tight ring of muscle. The pressure increased as it held out but then gave way. Ethan's swollen knob forced open my ass lips which slid down over his flared cock head, over its ridge and tightly snapped shut around his shaft. Both Ethan and I gasped with pleasure as his knob entered my ass.

Once his knob breached my sphincter he briefly held it there to savour having my hot, wet tight ass clamped around it. I flexed my ass muscles on it a couple of times which made his wonderfully sexy, tanned face scrunch up in intense pleasure. He then caught me totally by surprise and slammed his hot, hard, throbbing 7-inch cock deep into my hole. His densely pubed groin loudly slapped up against my pert upturned ass as his cock slammed deep into my ass. I gasped at having his chopper punch open the sensitive walls of my love chute as his shaft stretched and stimulated my ass ring. When he bottomed out in my ass he didn't hold it there instead he started pulling back.

He pulled back until just his swollen knob was in my ass. He then launch straight into a fast, rough, hard passionate fucking frenzy. At first, I was totally taken by surprise at the rough passion of his fucking. I was in a daze from having this fit sexy guy pound my tight ass so hard. His cock was a blur as he smashed it in my ass, his shaft making my ass lips glowing with friction. His swollen knob was forcing open and caressing the sensitive walls of my ass and due to our position, his knob rubbed against the front walls of my ass and bumped my prostate.

It took me a few minutes to come to my senses and adjust to the brutal fucking Ethan was giving me. He had never fucked me this hard before so something had really turned him on. His gorgeous face was scrunched up with the exertion he was using to pile drive his hot throbbing 7-inch cock ball deep into my pussy boy ass. We were both grunting and groaning with the intensity of the fuck. I was laid on my back with Ethan above me. My ankles were resting on his shoulders and his arms were supporting his upper body with a grip on the tool chest either side of me. His tanned arm, shoulder and chest muscles were tensed as they took the weight of his upper body. Already beads of sweat were starting to pop out on his sexy, toned upper body. He was supporting the weight of his lower body on his feet pressed against the van floor so that he was in a kind of push up position above me. I reached up and began to caress his tensed arms, grope his toned, sweaty chest, and pinch his dark brown nipples with the light dusting of hairs around them.

As Ethan fucked me I admired his fit, tanned sweaty body above me. His face looked even sexier than normal as expressions of intense sexual pleasure and physical exertion played across it. The sight of his tanned, tensed upper body was so sexy and the feel of it under my exploring hands felt so good. The smell of gay sex and man sweat mingled with the smell of tools and oil in the back of the van. My buttocks were ringing from the rapid and repeated slaps of his densely pubed groin against them. My ass lips felt swollen, puffy, and sensitive from the friction of his hot hard cock rapidly rubbing against them. The walls of my teen boy cunt were throbbing from repeatedly being rammed open by his tool. Each time he rammed his cock up me his knob bumped my prostate, which made my hard cock twitch on my stomach, leaving snail trails of pre-cum on it as it bounced about.

I was in sexual heaven at being fucked so rough, hard, and passionately by such a fit sex 23-year-old guy in the back of a builder's van, with his boyfriend and my fuck buddy watching. My ass was on fire with the pleasure of being fucked so fast and hard and my cock was throbbing away like mad. Both Ethan and I were loudly moaning and groaning in sexual pleasure as Ethan seemed to fuck me harder and harder. As he did so I flexed my ass muscles on his thrusting cock which had the desired result of making him fuck me faster and harder. I also told him how good it felt being fucked by him as well as begging for it harder.

I don't know how long Ethan fucked me for but it felt like ages and my ass was sure feeling it but in a good way. It felt tender and throbbing with each thrust of Ethan's hot hard cock, ball deep into it, sending waves of pleasure through me. I was moaning like the teen boy slut I was, eagerly taking the passionate fucking, this 23-year-old was giving me. I flexed my ass muscles on his pounding cock, increasing the pleasure and stimulation for both of us.

Ethan then slipped into a fucking frenzy and started pounding my tender ass faster and harder than before. We both began moaning and groaning louder at the increased passion and pace. My ass really was on fire with hard fucked pleasure now. His cock was a blur as he slammed it in and out of me. The walls of my love chute and ass lips were glowing from the friction of his sexy 7-inch cock sawing in and out of my boy pussy. His densely pubed groin was loudly slapping against my ass as he raced to orgasm. It was obvious Ethan was on the vinegar strokes and would come any moment now. Arnold also seemed to pick up on this and climbed over the seat and into the back of the van. I was half aware of Arnold peeling off his tee shirt, dropping his shorts and slowly stoking his hard cock as he watched his flat mate fuck me. I was only half aware of what Arnold was doing as I was concentrating more on the fit sexy guy above me fucking me senseless.

The faster and harder Ethan fucked me the faster and harder I worked my ass muscles on his pounding cock. I gripped it as tight as possible when he slammed his cock into me and relaxed it when he pulled out so that my ass sucked and closed after his retreating cock. I also groped his sweaty chest and pinched his lightly haired nipples faster and harder as he raced to orgasm. His fucking pace then reached fever pitch, his swollen knob slamming opens the throbbing walls of my love chute as his shaft set my sphincter on fire with pleasurable friction. "I'm close." Ethan gasped his gorgeous, tanned, freckled faced scrunched up with the pleasure and exertion of the fuck along with the desperate battle against the impending orgasm.

Ethan managed to last out for a minute or so more before I felt him slam his cock ball deep into my ass. I felt his cock throb, swell and pulse in my ass as with a loud grunt of pleasure he started blasting jet after jet of hot cum deep into my willing ass. Ethan loudly grunted and groaned with pleasure as I purred with delight as he filled my tender throbbing boy cunt with his hot cum. I felt every throb of his cock and every bolt of his cum squirt deep into my ass. I wildly flexed my ass muscles on his cock to fuel his orgasm and milk him dry. Ethan bucked and shuddered against me as he drained his balls into my young but experienced ass.

When Ethan finished cumming he sagged against me but Arnold gave him no time to recover. He practically pulled Ethan off me, his cock plopping out of my tender cum filled ass. Arnold at once adopted the position that Ethan had just vacated. I was still in a pleasurable daze from the fucking Ethan had just given me when Arnold got into position above me. I took in the sight of his handsome face, tanned muscular arms and shapely hairy chest. Like Ethan had done before he supported the weight of his upper body with his left arm on the tool chest. His right hand had a grip on his tanned, thick manly 7-inch cock which he was rubbing up and down my sweaty smooth ass crack as he searched out my swollen ass lips.

Arnold soon located the entrance to my ass and pressed his firm dick against it. Arnold didn't have any lube on his cock instead relying on the lube and cum from Ethan's fuck. I gasped in pleasure and mild pain as Arnold rammed open my tender ass lips with his swollen knob. As soon as his knob breached my ass ring he powerfully slammed his hot, hard, thick, throbbing, manly cock into my ass hole. I felt Ethan's cum bubble around Arnold's cock as he slammed it deep into me. I grunted at the rough power of the thrust Arnold had used to slam his cock deep into my tender ass. Arnold grunted with satisfied domineering pleasure as he impaled my cummy teen boy ass on his cock in one rough, deep, hard powerful thrust. He held his cock ball deep in my ass briefly to savour my young cum filled ass clamped around his cock.

Arnold then began to fuck me as rough hard and passionately as Ethan had done. My ass was already throbbing and tender from the passionate fucking Ethan had given it and after no rest it was taking another hard fucking. I certainly wasn't complaining, in fact it was the opposite. Yes, there was the occasional stab of pain or discomfort but that was far overridden by the throbbing pleasure of being fucked fast and hard. Both Arnold and I started loudly grunting and groaning with pleasure as he powerfully slammed his manly cock into my pussy boy ass. I felt his hard prick punching open the throbbing, tender, cum coated walls of my ass as he slammed it ball deep into me. As his cock was slightly thicker than Ethan's it was stretching my ass lips wider, increasing the stimulation on them.

As Arnold pounded away at my ass I looked up to admire the hunky man above me. I took in his tanned, handsome face which was framed by centre parted dark blond hair. Expressions of pleasure and exertion played across it, making it seem even sexier. His steely blue eyes stared down at me, the willing teen boy slut beneath him. My gaze also took in the sight of his tanned bulging arm and shoulders muscles. I got occasional glimpses of his tanned, toned hairy chest as I ran my fingers through its dark blond brown hairs of pinched and tugged his dark brown nipples. His washboard, lightly haired stomach also ripped as he slammed his manly cock into me.

As Arnold fucked me I flexed the muscles of my cummy ass around his pounding cock. I could feel Ethan's cum bubble around Arnold's cock as he thrust it in and out of me. Arnold's cock stretched my sphincter and love chute a bit wider than Ethan's cock had, sending waves of pleasure through me. His swollen knob also repeatedly bumped my prostate as he drove it deep into me, my stomach soaked in my own pre-cum as my cock wildly throbbing away. "Yeah take my cock, you dirty little slut." Arnold growled as he continued his rough relentless fucking. All through our fuck he talked dirty to me which really tuned me on and the fact he was dominating a slim, lean teen also really seemed to turn him on.

Arnold pounded away at my ass for at least as long as Ethan had. My boy cunt was now really throbbing and tender from all the fucking it had taken and I knew I still had one more cock to go. The feeling wasn't painful even though it was tender and sensitive. It is hard to explain how good your ass feels when being fucked rough and hard. My ass certainly was on fire with hard fucked pleasure, the walls of my love chute tender and throbbing. My ass lips felt swollen, puffy, and tender, glowing with the friction of having a hunky 27-year-old man's 7-inch cock stretching and rubbing against them. My buttocks were also lightly stinging from the repeated slaps of first Ethan's and then Arnold's pubed groin against them.

I was lost in the sexual pleasure of it all. I admired the fit sexy body of the hunky man above me as I felt the steeliness of his tensed muscles beneath my exploring hands. His hot, sweaty, manly aroused smell filled my nostrils as beads of sweat dropped off his body and onto mine. My cock was wildly throbbing and drooling pre-cum all over my flat smooth stomach as the cum boiled in my balls. Each thrust of his manly cock into my ass had my prostate being dumped and the walls of my ass rubbed. My ass lips were stretched and stimulated by his hot, thick throbbing shaft as he drove it deep into my cummy ass. The fact that I was an

18-year-old pussy boy being gang banged in the back of a works van by three men was also highly erotic and stimulating.

If I thought Arnold had been fucking me fast and harder to start with that was nothing compared to when he slipped into his pre-orgasm fucking frenzy. From somewhere he dug into strength reserves and started fucking my ass faster and harder than before. I began to see stars from being fucked so fast, rough, and hard. Arnold started calling me names as he raced towards orgasm. I just moaned and groaned with the pleasure and exertion of the fucking Arnold was giving me, squirming about underneath him.

As Arnold fucked me Ethan and Ronald had swapped positioned. Arnold was in his fucking frenzy as Ronald peeled off his tee shirt and dropped his shorts. He then came over to me and started slapping his really thick, pale, sexy, 8.5-inch cock against my lips. I twisted my head slightly to the left and opened my mouth. Ronald immediately pushed his large swollen cut knob into my mouth. I tightly clamped my lips around his thick, throbbing shaft just below the prominent ridge of his swollen knob. I then began to greedily suck and lick away at his knob as Arnold pounded my ass. Ronald reached down and started very roughly pinching and tugging my left nipple, rapid making it swell and become red, tender, and puffy. I muffled a moan of half pain, half pleasure around his cock at having my nipple roughed up in such a way. Ronald then started forcing more and more of his impressive cock into my mouth. His thick shaft stretched my lips and jaw to the max as the swollen knob plugged the back of my throat. He managed to force about 6 inches out of the 8.5 inches cock into my mouth before he maxed it out. I couldn't physically take any more of his cock into my mouth. Ronald held it there and I sucked on it. He then pulled it back until just his knob was in my mouth which I greedily sucked on. Ronald then began thrusting about the top 3 inches of his thick cock in and out of my mouth as Arnold fucked me from the other end.

This went on for a couple of minutes, Ronald fucking my mouth with his big thick cock as Arnold fucked my ass with his. I savoured the taste of Ronald's strong pre-cum on my tongue as I drank in his sweaty manly smell. I felt his hot thick cock stretch and rub my lips and slide over my tongue. I admired the sight of his thick, pale, sexy, 8.5-inch cock as he gently thrust it in and out of my cock hungry mouth. At the other end Arnold's fucking was reaching fever pitch. My ass really was throbbing and glowing with hard fucked pleasure. His swollen penis was punching open the tender cummy walls of my ass, his thick shaft stretching and stimulating my tender ass ring.

I felt so horny and slutty being used at both ends by two sexy fit men, taking one cock in my mouth and the other up my ass. I knew it would be short lived though as the way Arnold was fucking me he was on the brink of orgasm. Sure enough Arnold slammed his cock in and out of my throbbing boy cunt a few more times before he slammed it home one last time. I felt his sweaty, densely pubed groin slap up against my ass, his pubes tickling my swollen tender ass ring. I felt his thick manly cock swell, throb, and pulse inside me as it started powerfully blasting jet after jet of hot man spunk deep into my already cummy ass.

Arnold loudly cried out in pleasure as he powerfully orgasmed. I muffled moans of pleasure around Ronald's big thick cock as Arnold fired his spunk into me at the other end. He bucked and shuddered against me as if trying to drive more of his cock into me even though he was already buried up to the pubed hilt. I felt every throb of his cock and every squirt of his hot cum as he fired it deep into me, adding to the load that Ethan had already fired up there.

From the amount of cum Arnold fired in to me it was obvious that he'd been hyper horny from watching his teen boy slut being used by one of his work mates before him. When his orgasm ended he pulled his cock out from my tender and battered, but satisfied ass. I watched as he and Ronald swapped positions. Ronald got into position and I rested my ankles on his shoulders as I watched him grip his thick impressive cock and aim it at my ass. I felt him press his swollen, bulbous cut knob against my ass and start forcing it in. Although my ass ring was still tight it was now very malleable and opened easily to accept Ronald's large swollen knob. I felt my tender ass lips slide down over his flared knob and over its thick ridge. Then they tightly clamped shut around his very thick shaft.

Ronald held his knob just inside me, savouring having my hot, wet, tight ass clamped around it. I looked up at Ronald and saw his eyes were half closed in pleasure. His face wasn't as sexy as Arnold's or Ethan's but it was hot in a kind of rough almost chavy way. I saw the muscles in his pale arms standing out as they supported the weight of his upper body. My hands reached up and began caressing the tensed muscles in his arm. As I did so Arnold stood over me and dangled his spent cock, which was glistening with his and Ethan's cum and my ass juice, over my mouth. Without hesitation I took Arnold's slimy cock into my mouth and began greedily sucking it clean of his and Ethan's cum and my ass juice. The taste wasn't gross as there was no shit, instead it was kind of salty, earthy, and very nice.

I don't know if they planned it this way but Arnold offering me his cock had distracted me. While my attention was on sucking Arnold's cock clean Ronald powerfully rammed his very thick, 8.5-inch cock ball deep into my tender ass. Having such a long, thick, meaty cock rammed up my ass so fast and hard caught me totally by surprised and was quite painful. I tried to cry out in pain but Arnold strangled it before forcing his cock further into my mouth. My eyes bulged and watered as a sharp searing pain radiated out from my swollen, tender sphincter. Ronald's cock had it and my tender, cum filled love chute stretched to the max.

Ronald's cock was the biggest cock I had taken so far and my ass struggled to take it.

Ronald held me impaled on his cock, savouring feeling my hot, wet, tight, cummy ass clamped around it. Arnold held his cock in my mouth, muffling my pants as I fought the searing pain in my ass. However, Ronald didn't hang around for long. He held his cock briefly in my ass before he slowly pulled it back until the thick, prominent ridge of his large, swollen cut knob butted up against the inside of my tender ass ring. He then powerfully slammed all 8.5 thick throbbing inches ball deep into my ass. I felt Ethan's and Arnold's cum bubble around Ronald's meaty cock as his groin slapped up against my ass. Again, I gasped in pain and saw stars at having my tender, young ass penetrated so rough and hard by such a big thick cock. "Fuck him hard." Arnold instructed Ronald and at that point I knew I was in for a serious fucking.

No sooner has Arnold given the command than Ronald started slamming his monster cock in and out of my tight ass at break neck speed. I muffled moans of pain around Arnold's cock as his well-hung house mate pounded my boy cunt. Each thrust of his thick cock sent twinges of searing pain radiating throughout my ass. However, this pain was dented when his large, swollen knob hit my prostate, bringing a brief respite of pleasure. I squirmed about as I struggled to back away from Ronald's big cock. However, I was totally pinned down and knew there was no escape. Instead I fought to relax my ass and battled against the painful feelings radiating out from it, while trying to concentrate on the pleasure of his knob bumping my prostate.

Ronald knew the best way to fuck guys with his big, thick cock was to fuck them fast and hard until they past the pain barrier and that is exactly how he fucked me. For a couple of minutes, I was totally stunned by the painful overstuffed feeling radiating out from my already very tender, sensitive, well fucked ass. It had already taken two rough, hard passionate fucks in a row and now it was taking a third, but from a much longer and thicker cock. However, each deep, rough, hard, powerful thrust of Ronald's big cock into my ass became less painful and more pleasurable.

Gradually my tender, throbbing young ass began to adjust to being penetrated so rough and deep by such a thick cock. My muffled cries of pain became murmurs of pleasure around Arnold's cock. I felt Ronald's large swollen knob, with its thick ridge, ramming open the sensitive walls of my cummy ass and bumping my prostate as he drove it deeper into my ass than any cock before. His really thick shaft stretched my ass lips to the max, setting them on fire with pleasurable friction as he thrust his big cock in and out of me. His groin also loudly slapped against my pert, upturned ass as he grunted and groaned with the pleasure and exertion of fucking a teen boy. My ass felt so sore, over stretched, and full of cock which, although at times was uncomfortable, bordering on painful, it was also intensely pleasurable. I felt like such a slut at having my ass used by three men in a row and this just made me hornier.

As Ronald pounded away at my ass Arnold pulled his cock from my mouth once I'd sucked it clean. He started getting dressed as he watched his teen boy bitch being used by his well hung flat mate. He was egging Ronald on the whole time, telling him to fuck me like the teen tart I was and to really give me a good seeing to with his big, thick cock. I don't think Ronald needed much encouragement as he was a natural rough, passionate, aggressive top to start with, more so now that he was fucking a slim, lean teen boy. As he fucked me I looked up at his mean but sexy face with expressions of pleasure and exertion playing across it. His steely blue eyes were half closed as he savoured ramming his big, thick 8.5-inch cock ball deep into the cum filled ass of an 18-year-old boy. My hands swarmed all over and caressed his pale, tensed, toned arm and shoulder muscles, feeling their strength under my exploring fingers. I also groped his pale chest, ran my fingers through the small matt of soft dark hairs between his pecs and pinched and tugged on his pink nipples until they became red and puffy.

By now there was only the occasional stab of pain radiating out from my ass. The rest of the time it was throbbing and on fire with well fucked pleasure. His large, swollen, cut knob was forcing open and caressing the cum covered walls of my throbbing, tender ass. Each time he rammed his cock in he bumped my prostate, causing the cum to boil in my balls and made my cock throb and twitch on my pre-cum coated stomach. His thick, throbbing shaft had my ass lips stretched to the max, stimulating them as he thrust his manly cock ball deep into me. Arnold's & Ethan's cum bubbled around his thick pounding cock, some of which escaped from my ass and dribbled down. My buttocks were lightly stinging from having three groins slapped against them in a row.

I was deliriously squirming about and loudly moaning in intense sexual pleasure. Having my ass gang banged by three hunky guys in a row was really getting to me. My cock had hardly been touched, apart from the brief sucking Ethan had given it, yet I was on the brink of orgasm. Feeling three manly cocks pounding away at my ass one after the other and bumping my prostate really brought me to the boil. There wasn't just the physical pleasure of being relay fucked, there was also the erotic though that I was only 18 yet acting like such a slut to three sexy older guys. On top of that was the heady smell of men on boy gay sex mingling with the smell of their work van.

Each slam of Ronald's big, thick, meaty cock into my throbbing, tender ass brought me close and closer to orgasm. I fought against the rising pressure in my balls in a bid to stave off my orgasm as long as possible and therefore increase its intensity. It was a losing battle though as the hard-fucked pleasurable feelings radiating out from my ass and the repeated strikes of my prostate all became too much. I felt Ronald thrust his cock deep into my ass. His thick shaft stretched and stimulated my swollen, tender ass lips. His large, swollen, cut knob punched open the throbbing, sensitive walls of my pussy boy ass and bumped against my prostate. This was the final trigger. I arched my back and loudly cried out in ecstasy. The warning tingle in my groin intensified before I felt a bolt of cum race down my throbbing cock and explode all over me. The first jet was so powerful it splashed on my face and immediately my tongue darted out to lap up my thick, tasty cum. The second jet of cum also splashed on my face and I licked it up as the remaining four jets splashed all over my sweaty, heaving chest and stomach.

I loudly moaned and groaned in ecstasy as I covered myself in cum. The rough, hard, powerful fucking Ronald was giving me with his thick, meaty 8.5-inch cock fuelled and intensified my orgasm. As he carried on pounding his cock into my ass his knob repeatedly hit my prostate which made me cum even more. Waves of sexual pleasure flowed through my young body as I totally succumbed to my orgasm, lost in an orgasmic daze. My ass spasmed uncontrollable around Ronald's thick, pounding cock as I weakly shot the last of my load onto my stomach.

Even when I finished cumming, I was still on an intense sexual high, savouring the pleasure only a gang banged orgasm can produce. On top of the pleasure of orgasming the pleasurable feeling of Ronald's big thick cock slamming in and out of my ass was also making itself felt. My orgasm also seemed to have spurred him on as well. I felt him pick up his pace and fucked my now very tender, throbbing ass even faster and harder than before. My orgasm had made my well used ass even more sensitive and receptive to the rough, hard fucking Ronald was giving it. The wild spasms of my ass had also really turned Ronald on which pushed him into the fucking frenzy.

I gasped and grunted at the renewed vigour Ronald was using to fuck my ass. It was now hyper sensitive and struggling to take the frantic fucking it was receiving. However, it wasn't painful instead it was more like when your knob gets hyper sensitive after cumming. I felt every inch of his big, thick, throbbing cock slam in and out of my throbbing, tender ass and as I began to recover from my orgasm I began flexing and tightly gripping my ass muscles on his pounding cock. Ronald groaned with pleasure at the increased stimulation on his cock. His pale, toned body was glistening with sweat from the exertion of fucking me hard as mine glistened with my sweat and cum.

The feeling of my hot, wet, tight, cum filled ass wrapped around his big, thick cock like a velvet glove really started getting to Ronald. The soft, well walls of my ass rubbed and caressed his swollen, circumcised knob as my ass lips wanked his thick shaft. I tightly gripped my ass muscles on his cock when he thrust it deep into me and relaxed them when he pulled out. The feeling of Ethan's and

Arnold's cum bubbling around his cock also added to the pleasurable feelings radiating down his cock. All this built up until it reached critical mass.

Ronald was powerfully fucking my ass, his cock a blur as he impaled me on it. I then felt him slam it ball deep into me one last time. He threw his head back and loudly cried out his pleasure. I felt his already thick cock swell even more as the first bolt of cum raced down it and exploded deep into my already cummy ass. I purred with pleasure as I felt him pump his hot cum deep into my ass, bubbling around his thick cock which he is bucking and jerking about inside me. Ronald sure made a lot of noise when he came and he sure wasn't holding back now. Each blast of cum into my ass had him yelping with pleasure as he bucked against me. At the same time, I wildly flexed my ass muscles on his cock to fuel his orgasm and milk him dry.

From the amount of cum he fired into me it felt as if he hadn't cum in a week. When his orgasm faded he held his big cock deep in my truly battered, tender ass. He stayed like that for a minute or so as I flexed my ass on his spent cock. He then pulled it from my ass and I realised just how sore, throbbing, tender and sensitive it felt. Despite that it was already starting to miss feeling a hot hard cock up it. There was also a great deal of pleasure and it felt very satisfied and full of man spunk. Arnold threw me a rag and I cleaned my spunk off me, when I noticed another car standing about 10 meters away. I looked carefully and saw that someone had a camera and was filming us. Arnold noticed the look on my face and looked towards the car and saw the camera.

"Hey" Arnold shouted at the people in the car, and started driving towards them. The guys in the car noticed that we saw them and started driving away. Arnold drove the van as fast as he could, but they were already far away, and were able to disappear. None of us knew who these guys were, and if they could actually film us.

They dropped me off down the road from college. I only just managed to get back in time for my afternoon class. All through the afternoon, I stood in class with a throbbing, sore, well fucked ass, the cum of three sexy men leaking out and staining the crotch of my trackies. The crotch of my underwear became well soaked and crusty. My mind was thinking if we have actually been filmed, and who were these people were.

13.

After being relay fucked by Arnold, Ronald, and
Ethan, in the back of their work van, and
suspecting that we were filmed, I became really
nervous on the consequences of this. For a week, I
did not meet Arnold or his roommates, and only
saw them in class. After it has been over a week,
Arnold phoned and asked me to come over for sex
as Ronald and Ethan would be out that evening.
He assured me that the filming was from a
distance and they couldn't pick my face, and there
was nothing to worry about.

So, at the allotted time I went over to their house
and knocked on the door. Arnold answered it
wearing just a pair of footie shorts and I just had
to admire his sexy body. He had a handsome face
framed with dark blond hair that was parted in the
centre and bright blue eyes. My gaze then dropped
down to his golden tanned muscular chest which
was covered in blond brown hairs but not too hairy
to be a turn off. I also saw his tanned muscular
arms which I wanted wrapped around me. His
stomach was rock hard, rippled and covered in the
same dusting of blond brown hairs as his chest. I
checked out the front of his light blue footie shorts
and it didn't look like he had a boner yet.

When I stepped through the front door he told me
to go into the lounge which I did as he followed me.
When I stepped into the lounge there was an
opened bottle of red wine and a couple of glasses
on the coffee table with several scented candles

flickering away. It looked quite romantic and I felt happy that he'd gone to this much effort.

"Do you like?" Arnold asked.

"Yes." I said as I turned to face him and ran the fingers of my left hand through his mat of chest hairs, giving him a puppy love smile. He leant forward and as our lips locked we began to passionately kiss each other. To start with it was just our lips mashing against each other's but then he forced his tongue into my mouth. We tongued fenced before he battled mine into submission and I began to suck on his tongue. All the while we were doing this I was running both of my hands over his muscular, manly hairy chest and washboard stomach, my cock rapidly swelling in the confines of my trackie bottoms. It was nice feeling his strong chest under my exploring hands but they soon started homing in on his brown nipples which I began to rub. As I rubbed them they started to stiffen and as they stiffened I started pinching and tweaking them so that they became red and puffy.

For a couple of minutes, we kissed as I teased his nipples. Arnold then broke off our kiss to pull my tee shirt off over my head. Once I was bare chested we resumed our passionate kissing and Arnold began to caress my pale slim smooth upper body with his big rough builder's hands. Soon, like mine, his hands homed in on my nipples and began to roughly pinch and tug them; taking them to the pleasure/pain boarder and making them go red and puffy. Already I could feel our lust and passion bubbling away as we kissed each other and caressed each other's upper body. Arnold then lifted up his right arm and exposed his armpit. I knew exactly what he wanted so I broke off our kiss and dove straight into his hairy armpit which I began to eagerly lick out. It only vaguely tasted and smelt of sweat but I eagerly licked it out any way. After giving it a good tongue bath I kissed and licked my way to his right nipple which was already red and puffy from my pinching of it. I circled my tongue around it and felt goose bumps form. I then began flicking my tongue over his nipple before gently taking it between my teeth where I began to chew and tug on it making it even redder.

At the same time, I was pinching and tugging his left nipple. Soon I swapped nipples dragging my tongue through the hairs on his chest to reach his left nipple which I circled my tongue around before taking into my mouth to chew and tug on it. With my left hand I began pinch his right saliva soaked nipple. Arnold then lifted up his left arm and I moved over to lick it out. A couple of minutes later and Arnold placed his hands on my shoulders and started pushing me down. I let my knees bend and as I sank down I dragged my tongue down through the hairs on his chest and stomach. When I reached his groins, I was knelt before him, eye level with the obvious bulge in his footie shorts. I rubbed my hand up and down the length of his cock and felt its thick meatiness, warm throbbing pulse, and steely hardness through the material of his shorts.

I looked up and gave him a sexy smile which he repaid by placing a hand on the top of my head and grinding my face into his groin. I felt his hot, hard manly cock underneath the satiny material of his shorts rub against my face. I pursed my lips and allowed them to rub up and down the covered meaty length of his cock. His manly aroused aroma also started to filter through his shorts and fill my nose, fanning my flames of lust and passion still further. I surrendered to Arnold and allowed him to grind my face into his groin for as long as he wanted. When he released his grip on my head I pulled back slight and looked up to give him my best cock suckers grin as I hooked my fingers under the waistband of his shorts. I began to pull them down first exposing his dense bush blond brown pubes. As I pulled them further down, I started to expose the golden tanned, meaty, veiny shaft of his sexy cock. When I pulled his shorts past his knob his cock bounced about until if found its natural position. As I let his shorts drop to his ankles I admired his manly cock. He had a dense bush of blond brown pubes with big low hanging hairy balls. His cock was 7 inches long and uncut but when hard his foreskin peeled all the way back so that he almost looked cut. It was golden tanned, a nice thickness with prominent veins running down it.

After admiring his hot sexy cock, I took it in my left hand and felt its thick meaty girth and warm throbbing pulse as I gave it a couple of wanks. I then leant forward and began to lick away at his low hanging balls before licking one into my mouth where I sucked on it. As I did so his cock throbbed and twitched above my face and I looked up to admire it and saw Arnold looking down to watch me. I then let his ball fall from my mouth before I took in his other and gave it the same treatment. It wasn't long before the sight of his throbbing cock tempted me away from his balls. I flicked the base of his cock and couple of times before I dragged my tongue up the underside of his cock a bit and then back down. I kept repeating this but each lick became longer and travelled further up the underside of his cock. Soon I was almost reaching the sensitive underside of his knob where his foreskin joined but for a bit I teased him and always stopped short of it. However, when I saw a pearl of pre-cum form on the tip I dragged my tongue up the full length of his cock, over the sensitive area where his foreskin joined and then over his knob to lick up his pre-cum. My tongue savoured its taste before I started swarming it all over his swollen sensitive knob. Arnold purred with pleasure as I licked my tongue all over his knob, causing him to leak even more tasty pre-cum. I savoured the taste and spongy feel of his knob under my tongue as I drank in his manly aroused aroma. My hands were caressing all over his muscular hairy thighs or reaching around to grope his toned ass. I spent a couple of minutes just licking his knob or up and down his shaft before I licked my way to the tip of his cock which I kissed before forcing my mouth down on to it.

My moist lips parted and slid down his flared knob, over its ridge and clamped tight around his thick shaft. Arnold gasped with pleasure as his swollen, sensitive knob was engulfed in the hot wet mouth of a cock hungry boy. With his knob in my mouth I began to greedily suck it and swarm my tongue all over it, paying particular attention to the underside where his foreskin joined. Arnold purred with pleasure as he looked down to watch, his cock oozing pre-cum. I gave his knob a good working over, sucking and licking it, before I relaxed my throat and jaw and started forcing my mouth further down onto his cock. My tightly clamped lips rubbed his thick meaty shaft as my tongue licked and caressed the sensitive underside as I forced my hot, wet mouth further down onto his manly cock. Soon I had all 7 inches of his cock throbbing in my mouth, my nose buried in his dense blond brown pubes and his balls against my chin. Arnold gasped with pleasure as I swallowed all of his cock. I flexed my throat muscles on his swollen knob, which was plugging the back of my throat, as I flicked the base of his cock with my tongue.

When the urge to breathe kicked in I pulled my mouth back up his cock licking and sucking it as I did so. When I reached his knob, I sucked and licked it before working my mouth all the way back down onto his cock. "Yeah suck my cock." Arnold groaned as I swallowed him whole again. I didn't need to be told as my natural cock sucking instincts were already kicking in as I began to bob my hot, wet sucking mouth up and down the full length of his manly cock, deep throating him all the way. When his knob plugged the back of my throat I flexed the muscles there on it. As I bobbed my mouth up and down his cock I wanked it with my tightly clamped lips, sucked it and caressed it with my tongue. When I reached the tip I strongly sucked it and swarmed my tongue all over it before repeating the process.

For a few minutes I deep throated Arnold's sexy cock, taking it all the way in to the pubed hilt. However, when my jaw began to ache I pulled my mouth off his cock and licked up and down the sides and underside of it like a lollipop. I then took his knob back into my mouth and just sucked and licked away on it before starting to bob my mouth up and down his cock but only taking in half of it. I was really getting into sucking off this sexy hunky man and was feeling like such a slut for doing so. I was in cock suckers' heaven as I worked my mouth up and down his manhood and caressed his muscular hairy thighs with my hands.

I would have happily carried on sucking on his cock but he pushed me off. "That was fucking ace but it's too early to cum yet. Let's watch TV and have some wine." He said. I was disappointed at this because my natural teen horniness had increased tenfold from the pleasure of sucking on this sexy hunky man's cock and now he was denying me that pleasure. Reluctantly I agreed. I stood up and pushed down my bottoms releasing my raging cock that had been wildly throbbing away inside them during my sucking of Arnold's cock. I stepped out of them and my socks and sat beside Arnold who had already taken a place on the sofa. He poured us both a generous glass of red wine each and put on the TV. We watched TV with me snuggled against his muscular hairy chest with his right arm around me.

We spent a couple of hours like this and finished off the wine. It was then that I noticed Arnold's cock grow and become hard again. He then put his hand on the back of my head and pushed it down. As my face drew closer to his cock I opened my mouth and took the tip of his cock into it when I reached it. I heard Arnold gasp with pleasure and felt his cock throb as I began to suck and lick his knob. He briefly allowed me to do this before he used his grip on my head to force my mouth up and down his cock. He was totally in control of it and all I could do was relax my jaw and throat and go with it. Although he controlled how much of his cock he forced into my mouth I was still able to suck it and caress it with my tongue. Being used in this way and being totally under his control was highly erotic and stimulating for me. My cock was rock hard, wildly throbbing and drooling pre-cum. To start he was quite gentle and didn't force my mouth that far onto his cock but soon he started losing control and began forcing my mouth faster and further onto his cock. Soon he was forcing it all the way down to the pubed hilt and as he was in control of the blow job I had to fight my gag reflexes. I only just managed it but my eyes watered as this hunky man forced his cock deep into my mouth, his rod playing punch bag with my tonsils. He had a rough grip of my shaggy hair which was making my scalp sting as he used the grip to force my mouth up and down his manly cock. Even though it was slightly uncomfortable I was surprised to find myself highly turned on by this turn of events. I was totally under Arnold control and it excited me very much. I endured this for a couple of minutes before Arnold suddenly let go.

"Have you ever been tied up and fucked?" He asked. The thought of being tied up for sex had never occurred to me before but now that he mentioned it the thought of being even more helpless and under his control thrilled me. When I told him, I hadn't he told me to lie on his exercise bench. At on end of the bench were two upward struts which supported a weights bar. At the other end was an adjustable padded bar for ankles or knees depending upon the exercise you were doing. Arnold told me to get on it so that my feet were at the weights end and my head at the ankle bar end. Once I was laid on the bench he grabbed my ankles and pulled me along the bench so that my ass was on the edge under the weight bar. He then draped my ankles over the weights bars and told me to keep them there. He then went over to a draw and pulled out some strips of satin like material. He then went ahead to tie both my ankles to the weights bar. He then tied my wrists together and then tied these to the ankle bar that was above my head. To finish off he placed a sofa cushion under my head. I tugged on my bonds and found that I was tied fast with very little amount of movement. I knew I was now at Arnold's mercy but I trusted him not to hurt me and I found being tied up and helpless very exciting. My heart was racing, my stomach fluttering and my cock wildly throbbing with excitement and anticipation. This was a new and novel situation for me and I was enjoying it. The finishing touch was when he used another strip of silky material to gag my mouth. I twisted my head to the side and looked at my reflection in the mirror they had in the gym corner of the lounge. What I saw was a pale lean shaggy haired boy with his long slender legs and body forming a Z with my ankles tied to the cross bar and my part pale ass on the edge of the bench. My arms were tied together, pulled back over my head and tied to the ankle bar. My cute face was looked back at me, a red strip of silk gagging my mouth. I must admit it was a very erotic sight and I saw my cock throb and twitch at it.

Once I was tied up Arnold came over and started caressing my pale smooth flat chest. To start with it was loving and gentle but his caresses became shorter as he homed in on my nipples. I felt him circle his fingers around my nipples making goose bumps form around them and sending shivers through me. He then started rubbing them both between his fingers making them swell and stiffen. When my nipples reached full hardness, he began to pinch and tug on them gradually getting rougher with them. Soon he was really abusing them sometimes going past the pleasure/pain border and into pain. However, I was totally helpless and all I could do was muffle yelps of pain and fruitlessly strain against my bonds. For several minutes Arnold tortured my nipples before leaving them very sore, red, and swollen. He then caressed his way down my flat smooth stomach and circled his hands teasingly close to my throbbing cock. Arnold then went to the coffee table a pulled an ostrich feather out of a vase full of them.

He came over and began to tickle me with it starting with my armpits first. Now I'm very ticklish so I squirmed about like mad under the feather light tickle. Arnold then brought it down and lightly rubbed it over my sore sensitive nipples, which made goose bumps form around them again. Further down the tickling feather came, over my flat stomach which uncontrollably spasmed under it. Arnold then began to tickle my tight lightly pubed balls with it and then up and down my throbbing cock which was aching for more substantial stimulation. Arnold's teasing was driving me wild with lust and unsatisfied pleasure, made all the worse by the fact that I was tied up and totally helpless to do anything about it. Having the feather dragged up and down my throbbing cock was definitely the worst. It made the cum churn in my balls and I was desperate to firmly grab my cock in my hand and furiously beat it off until I spewed my hot spunk all over my body. However only I could do was take further teasing pleasure from Arnold and the ostrich feather.

Already I had snail trails of pre-cum over my stomach, charting the progress of my twitching cock over it. Arnold then brought the feather down to my ass and dragged it up and down the crack and tickled my sphincter with it. He really had me bubbling away with lust and passion and I didn't know how much more of this I could take. Luckily, I didn't have to endure it for much longer as Arnold dropped the feather and knelt down in front of my ass. I muffled a gasp of pleasure into my gag as I felt Arnold dragged his hot wet tongue from the base of my spine, up between my downy haired ass crack, over my sphincter and the sensitive bridge next to it before finishing by licking over my balls. I looked down and saw his handsome face surface from between my buttocks before he went back down and repeated the lick. I squirmed against my bonds, shivers of pleasure running through my prone body as Arnold expertly lapped away at my ass. Soon he was circling his tongue around my sphincter and then flicking over it. My pucker quivered under the onslaught of his tongue which he then started worming into my boy cunt, stabbing it in and out like a like cock. Arnold's tongue fucking of my ass added to my horniness, worming his tongue deep into me and tickling the walls of my love chute. As he was doing this he was greasing up his cock although I couldn't see it at the time.

After giving my ass a good tongue fucking, he stood up and that is when I saw his hard-throbbing cock glistening with lube. With his left hand he gripped the weights bar and with his right he aimed his cock at my ass and rubbed it up and down my crack until he found my asshole. I felt him nestle his swollen knob in the entrance to my ass. Then before I knew what was going on he grabbed the bar with his other hand and used his two-handed grip to lever himself forward. I cried out in pain into my gag as a sharp searing pain radiated out from my sphincter as Arnold's swollen knob brutally forced it open. My ass lips were rammed open and slid down over his flared knob and its thick ridge before clamping around his thick shaft.

However, that was only the start as soon as his knob had breached my ring piece he powerfully rammed the rest of his thick, throbbing cock ball deep into my ass. I saw stars and my body locked ridged as the pain of having my ass brutally penetrated flowed through my prone teen body. My ass was fire at being penetrated so fast and hard with the only respite being when his hard package bumped my prostate. I saw Arnold face scrunch up with the pleasure of roughly invading the steamy hot, tight confines of a teen boy's ass as his pubed groin loudly and firmly slapped up against my buttocks. He grunted with satisfied delight when he bottomed out in my stunned ass and held his cock ball deep in me, letting it throb and twitch. He only held his cock in me briefly before he pulled it all the way out again.

I felt my love chute sucking and closing after his retreating cock and then felt my stinging ass lips parted from the inside before snapping shut as he pulled the last of his cock from my ass. I gasped a sigh of relief but that was soon replaced by another muffled cry of pain as his swollen knob punched open my ass lips a second time and then forcing open the walls of my love chute as he powerfully rammed all his cock deep into me. I felt faint at being fucked so rough and hard yet there was nothing I could do about it as I was tied fast and gagged. Again, he briefly held his cock deep in me where he twitched and jerked it about before pulling it all the way out. Arnold then kept repeating it, pulling his cock all the way out of my ass before powerfully slamming it back in ball deep. Soon my ass lips felt very sore and swollen, the walls of my love chute throbbing with a dull ache. I was seeing stars and groaning at the rough, unbridled passion of the fuck Arnold was giving me.

Arnold fucked me like that for a couple of minutes and gradually my ass began to be fucked into submission and adjust to the rough hard fucking he was giving it. The pain began to fade to a dull throbbing ache, which in turn mellowed into pleasure. Arnold also stopped pulling his cock all the way out. Instead he pulled his cock back until the thick ridge of his knob butted up against my ass ring before he powerfully drove it ball deep into me again. With each thrust of his thick, meaty cock the pain in my ass turned to pleasure, although there was the occasional stab of pain. My sphincter was sore, sensitive, and glowing with the pleasurable friction of his thick shaft stretching and stimulating it. His swollen knob was punching its way deep into my boy cunt, making the walls of my love chute throb and spasm. Due to our position each time he thrust his cock in my ass his stiff tool bumped my prostate, which made the cum churn in my balls.

My buttocks started to mildly sting from the repeated slaps of his ass against them. As he raped my teen boy ass I looked up and saw the expressions of pleasure, exertion and domination playing across his handsome face as he looked down at the prone teenager before him. His arm muscles were tensed and flexing as he used his grip on the weights bar to pull himself in and out of my ass. His pecs were bulging under their covering of blond brown hairs, his firm hairy washboard stomach rippling away as he thrust his cock in and out of me. Now that I was adjusting to the roughness of the fuck I could take all this in. I also became aware of the increased smell of male pheromones and man on teen gay sex. I had totally been taken by surprise at the way Arnold had started fucking me and although it was pretty painful to start with I was beginning to enjoy it as my pussy boy nature took over. Arnold had now fucked my ass into submission and was continuing to liquidate it with his rapidly thrusting manly cock.

My sphincter was glowing and stretched to the match, the walls of my ass throbbing from the repeated blows of his swollen knob against them. My cock, which had wilted under the brutal onslaught of his initial fucking, had now swelled to its full hardness, and was throbbing on my stomach and oozing pre-cum. It was now that I was beginning to enjoy the fuck and from being used in this way. I was totally helpless and under Arnold's control which I found very erotic. The physical pleasure of having my cock-hungry ass rough fucked was added to be the sight of the tanned hunky guy towering above me, sweat starting to bead on his body.

Now that I had overcome the initial shock, I began to flex my throbbing ass muscles on Arnold's thick pounding cock. He grunted with the pleasure of feeling a slutty boy use his ass to grip his cock in a hot, wet, vice like grip. This increased the pleasure for both of us, Arnold loudly moaning with my moans being muffled by my gag. Arnold really was slamming away at my ass which was sore and tender yet on fire and throbbing with hard fucked pleasure, my prostate getting a serious working over from his swollen knob. I was so lost in the passion of our fuck that I only vaguely heard the front door close and voices travelling along the corridor.

The door to the lounge opened and in stepped Ronald and Ethan as expected. However, what I didn't expect was the third guy who came in with them. There I was bollock naked, tied to an exercise bench being fucked senseless by a hunky man and in walks another student of mine. When he saw me and the predicament I was in, a smile broke out across his face and he said something in Spanish or Portuguese. Despite being shocked and confused, not to mention mortally embarrassed, at being caught in such an intimate act by another student of mine, I couldn't help but remember him. He was in his early 20's with a sexy round Latino tanned face, with dark brown eyes and short wiry dark brown hair. Even with a lustful leer on his face, I could tell that he was sexy. He was wearing a white tee shirt and from the way it hugged his body I could tell that he was fit and hunky underneath it.

"Do you have a problem for someone to join us?" Ronald asked as he blatantly started stripping off. Even though I was shocked and confused with the situation I couldn't help but watch Ronald pull off his tee shirt and nodding with approval. First, he exposed his pale, firm washboard stomach with its light dusting of brown hairs. As he pulled his tee shirt up further he exposed his pale lightly toned chest, which had a small mat of brown hairs between his pecs and around his nipples. As he pulled it off completely I saw his pale lickable armpits, with their small tufts of brown hairs. I could see a lustful look on his sexy chavy face, which had a mean but sexy quality to it. His bluey grey eyes looked glazed so I guessed they'd just come from the pub.

I was only able to briefly admire Ronald's sexy, pale toned body as the new guy started pulling off his tee shirt and distracted my attention. As he lifted it up I saw his deeply tanned, firm stomach which was covered in a mat of brown hairs. This narrowed down as it travelled upwards so that his chest only had a light dusting between his pecs. His chest was tanned and sexily toned with big dark brown nipples. When he pulled his tee shirt off I saw his tanned lickable armpits had a dense patch of brown hairs in them. My suspicions were right and he did have a fit, sexy, hunky upper body with strong arms too and I began to realise I was going to be gang fucked by these four men. Of course, I wanted it, my slutty nature racing to the fore before doubt even had a chance to surface.

It was Ethan who distracted my attention next as he pulled off his tee shirt first exposing his tanned flat stomach which had a light dusting of blond brown hairs. He was quick and soon it was off over his head only allowing me a brief glimpse of his armpits which had blond brown hairs in them. Ethan too had a sexy upper body which was strong although it wasn't quite as defined as the others. By the time my attention returned to Ronald and the new guy, they were both down to their underwear which had obvious bulges down the legs of their boxers. They both kicked off their socks so I was able to admire their legs. Ronald's were pale, sexily toned and covered in dark brown hairs. The other guy's legs were even more toned and muscular with the same Latino tan as the rest of him and covered in brown hairs. He was turning out to be a very sexy guy indeed. Than Ethan stepped out of his jeans and I could admire his very sexy, strong, golden tanned, blond haired legs.

Now that all three of them were stripped down to their underwear they moved over to where Arnold was fucking me. All through the strip show, Arnold had continued his rough, relentless fucking of my ass concentrating on fucking me rather than the other three. Despite enjoying looking up to admire Arnold's fit, sweaty hunky body towering above me and watching the expressions of pleasure and exertion playing across his handsome face I now had some new entertainment and I couldn't help but twist my head to the side and watch. I saw Ronald and the new guy stood side by side as Ethan dropped to his knees in front of them. He pulled down their boxer shorts to reveal their cocks. Now I'd seen Ronald's big impressive cock a few times and I never tired of admiring it. It was as pale as the rest of him and hung down under its own thick meaty weight.

The new guy's cock was equally well endowed with a cock that looked the same length as Ronald's. However, the new guy's cock seemed a little thicker and was uncut. It was duskily tanned although his groin area was of a slightly lighter colour than the rest of him. He had a big pair of balls hanging under his impressive cock. I though my ass is sore as it is and if these two well hung guys are going to fuck me after Arnold and Ethan, I won't be able to sit down for a week. I watched as Ronald and the new guy began to caress each other's chest as Ethan leant forward and began sucking on the new guy's big thick cock. I couldn't see much except for the back of Ethan's blond head bobbing back and forth. Although the sex show Ronald, Ethan and the new guy were putting on had distracted my visual attention, my physical attention was still centred on the feelings radiating out from my roughly fucked ass.

Arnold was still pounding his thick, meaty 7-inch manly cock in and out of my throbbing, tender ass at break neck speed. His hard rod was punching open and rubbing the throbbing, bruised walls of my love chute. Each thrust had his knob bumping my prostate which made my throbbing hard cock drool more pre-cum onto my stomach. His thick shaft was stretching my swollen sensitive ass lips wide and making them glow with pleasurable friction. However, from the pace and passion he was using to fuck my ass and his laboured breathing I guessed that he was getting close to creaming in my battered ass.

For a couple more minutes, Arnold pounded my ass with rough, deep, hard, powerful thrusts. I switched my gaze from looking up at Arnold's sweaty hunky body and handsome face to looking over to watch Ethan taking it in turns to suck on Ronald's and then the new guy's cock. It was obvious that Arnold was now in a fucking frenzy, his face scrunched up with the exertion of the fuck and the strain of fighting back his orgasm. I could tell he was close so began flexing my sore, throbbing ass muscles on his cock even faster and harder than before. That was the final trigger. I felt Arnold slam his cock into me a couple more times before he rammed it home one last time. His groin loudly slapped against my buttocks as he buried his thick meaty cock ball deep into my tender ass. I felt it swell throb and pulse as he threw his head back, his face scrunching up in ecstasy. With a loud cry Arnold began blasting jet after jet of hot man spunk deep into my bruised battered teen boy cunt. I felt every throb of his cock and every jet of his hot cum coat the walls of my ass. I wildly flexed my ass muscles on Arnold's orgasming cock to milk him dry. Arnold bucked and shuddered against me, stabbing my ass with short thrusts of his cock, his handsome face contorted with sexual pleasure as he drained his ball into me. I muffled moans of pleasure as I felt my tender ass filling up with man spunk, which kind of soothed the sore walls of my ass. When Arnold finished cumming he held his cock deep in me as he caught his breath and I flexed my cummy ass muscles on it.

Arnold knelt and kissed me then said, "Who do you want next?" as he pulled his spent cock from my battered ass which felt sore, gapping open and full of cum.

"I reckon Ethan should go next." I replied because his cock was smaller than Ronald and the new guy's. Even so Ethan still had a very respectable 7-inch cock that was uncut, golden tanned and a nice thickness. Ethan seemed more than pleased with this as he pulled his sucking mouth off the new guy's cock. Ethan than stood up and walked towards me. As he did so I admired his fit sexy, all over tanned body. I took in his sexy, handsome face, blond hair, and hazel eyes. My gaze then dropped down to take in the sight of his golden tanned barrel chest and dark brown nipples surrounded by a few blond brown hairs. His arms were strong and tanned and his stomach was flat and firm with a light covering of blond brown hairs.

Although Ethan didn't have much muscles definition he certainly had strength. Ethan's golden tan went all over his sexy body including his ass, groin, and cock. As he walked towards me I saw his tanned cock swinging about, his balls acting like a pendulum underneath. I was also able to get a quick look at his very sexy, muscular shapely, golden haired legs before he stood at the end of the exercise bench I was tied to. He looked down at me and gave me a dirty smile as he gripped his cock in his right hand and aimed it at my ass. I felt him rub his knob up and down my sweaty ass crack as he searched my ass that Arnold had already fucked open and greased with lube and man spunk.

When Ethan located my sore swollen ass lips, I felt him press his knob against them. He increased the pressure and they offered little resistance, instead parting, and sliding down over his flared knob as he pushed more and more of it into my ass. They slipped over the ridge of his knob and clamped around his shaft. He then continued to force his cock into me, his swollen knob forcing open the throbbing cum coated walls of my ass. Whereas Arnold had fucked me fast and hard right from the start, Ethan was slowly forcing his cock into me, savouring the feeling of sinking his cock into the cum filled confines of a tied-up boy.

As his knob travelled deeper into my ass I felt Arnold's cum bubble around Ethan's cock head as his shaft stretching and rubbing my sensitive ass lips. All the while he slowly forced his cock into my battered young ass he had a sexy smile on his face as he lustily looked down at me. When he bottomed out in my ass he held his throbbing cock ball deep in me and I flexed my ass muscles on it. Movement out of the corner of my eye caught my attention and I turned to see Arnold knelt and from the way his head was bobbing back and forth I could tell he was sucking on the new guy's cock. The new guy and Ronald were still caressing each other's upper body with the new guy using his other hand to wank Ronald's cock.

Ethan then started slowly pulling his cock out of my cummy ass and I felt it sucking and closing after his retreating cock. He pulled back until the ridge of his knob butted up against the inside of my ass ring before he slowly forced all back into me. He then broke into a nice slow, steady fuck, penetrating my ass with long slow, deep thrusts of his cock. As he did so I looked up to admire his sexy face with its look of pleasure and to take in the sight of his tanned, lightly haired stomach rippling, his chest and arm muscles tensed as he gripped the weights bar to give himself leverage.

After the rough hard fucking Arnold had given me Ethan's slower and gentler fuck was a relief. My ass was still sore and tender but it was enjoying feeling Ethan's hot, hard cock slowly thrusting in and out of it. My sphincter was glowing with the pleasurable friction of his shaft stretching and rubbing it. His groin rhythmically slapped against my buttocks whenever he bottomed out in my ass. There were two downsides to being tied up as I was. The first was that my hands were not free to caress and roam all over Ethan's sexy upper body as they wished. Also, the whole situation had made me hornier than I'd ever been before. My cock was screaming out for attention but I couldn't give it any and it seemed no one else intended to either. But on the flip side this helplessness was also very arousing which just sent the whole thing into a vicious circle.

This was further heightened when Ethan started fucking me faster and harder. Although he started off slow and gentle he soon began to pick up the pace with each thrust of his cock. I muffled moans of pleasure into my gag as I felt Ethan's hot hard cock thrust in and out of my ass faster and harder. I began to grip it tight with my ass muscles increasing the pleasure for both of us. Each thrust of his cock ball deep into me sent a wave of pleasure through my body and when his knob bumped my prostate my cock twitched and oozed more pre-cum as the pressure in my balls intensified. I was in pussy boy heaven from being tied up and relayed fucked. Already I was on my second fuck and I knew I had at least two more to go.

Ethan gave me a good fucking, gradually getting faster and harder, setting my ass on fire with hard fucked pleasure. When I felt his fucking pace quicken still further and his breathing become faster and more laboured I could tell he was getting close to orgasm. Instinctively my ass began flexing its muscles on Ethan's pounding cock even faster. His erect dick was rapidly forcing open the throbbing walls of my tender ass, Arnold's cum bubbling around it, some of which had already escaped my ass, trickling down my crack. His sexy face was rippling with expressions of pleasure and enjoyment as he fucked my ass good and hard. The lust and passion of our fuck was reaching its intensity and although I was really enjoying the fuck I was eager to feel him orgasming in my ass.

Ethan looked down at me his eyes burning with lust as he smashed his cock in my ass. I then felt him slam it ball deep into me and his face scrunched up as I felt his cock swell, throb, and pulse deep in me. Ethan began to loudly grunt and groan as he started blasting hot cum deep into my pussy boy ass. I muffled moans of pleasure as I felt a second load of man cum being fired into me. It felt so good feeling Ethan's hot cum bubbling around his rod head and coating the walls of my ass. Ethan bucked and shuddered with the throes of orgasm as he drained his balls into me. When he finished he held his cock deep in me and I flexed my ass muscles on it as it slowly went soft and plopped from my ass.

He then went over to the sofa and plopped down exhausted. I twisted my head to the side to see who was next. I saw Arnold stood bent at the waist with Ronald fucking his ass as the new guy fucked his mouth. Once Ronald saw that Ethan had finished with my ass a lustful grin spread across his face. I saw Ronald pull his big thick cock out of Arnold's ass and saw it sway in front of him as he walked over to me. Despite my ass feeling sore, tender, and used, I knew I was about to receive a rough hard fucking from a big cock and I was looking forward to it. I took in the sight of Ronald's pale fit body as he walked towards me but my gaze soon returned to his big cock that I knew he would be soon ramming up my ass.

When Ronald reached me, he stood at the foot of the exercise bench and with his right hand he aimed his thick meat cock at my ass. He shuffled forward and I felt him pressed his swollen cut knob against my sore, swollen ass lips. The pressure increased and then with a slight stinging pain they parted and slid down over his flared knob. Ronald's cock was thick with a big swollen knob so it forced open my ass lips more than Arnold's or Ethan's cocks had. They were further stimulated as he slowly forced the rest of his thick tool into my ass. I felt his swollen knob forcing open the bruised walls of my ass with Arnold's and Ethan's cum bubbling around it. His thick throbbing shaft stretched and stimulated my tender sphincter until he buried all his impressive cock into me. When he bottomed out he held his cock ball deep in me where he savoured the hot, wet, tight cummy confines of my teen boy ass. He jerked his cock about inside me and I felt it throb and twitch. I began to flex my ass muscles on his thick cock which made him gasp with pleasure. I knew this was the calm before the storm as Ronald was a rough passionate fucker.

"You look so hot tied up like that." He said as he took in the sight of my slim, lean, naked body tied up tight to the exercise bench.

"It's a good job you are such a dick loving slut because we are going to gang fuck you senseless." He added and with that he pulled his cock almost all the way out until the thick ridge of his cock butted up against the inside of my ass ring. Then with a grip on the weights bar that made the muscles on his arms tense and bulge he powerfully rammed his cock inside me. I muffled a cry of pleasure/pain into my gag at taking such an impressive cock so fast and hard up my already tender well fucked ass. Ronald just grunted with the exertion and pleasure of forcing his big cock into the cum filled ass of a pussy boy, a look for enjoyment and pleasure on his face. With that he started slamming his big, thick dick in and out of my ass rough and hard. Right from the start he thrust it in fast, hard, and deep making sure he got maximum penetration so that his groin loudly slapped against my buttocks as his large, swollen knob tickled parts of my ass no cock had reached before. Within seconds my ass was on fire and throbbing with hard fucked pleasure, my ring piece glowing with the friction of his thick shaft stretching and stimulating it. He was really testing the cock taking abilities of my ass, causing me to see stars.

"Yeah, professor. take my chopper, you dirty little bitch." Ronald grunted which added to my horniness. Some may think it weird but I get seriously turned on by being talked dirty to or insulted when I get fucked. Arnold and Ethan didn't do it much to me but Ronald would really lay into me and when coupled with his big cock and rough hard fucking really made me feel like a pussy boy whose sole purpose was to be used like a whore. As he fucked me I'd feel the occasional stab of pain when he thrust his big cock into me at a different angle. Apart from that my ass was feeling so good at being fucked so hard by such a long, meaty cock.

The walls of my ass throbbed with pleasure each time his knob forced them open, Arnold's and Ethan's cum squelching around it. My sphincter was tightly gripping his thick shaft, which was stretching it to the max and making it glow red with pleasurable friction. Each thrust of his tool ball deep into me had his large swollen knob bumping my prostate which had already received a serious working over from Arnold's and Ethan's fucks. Now it was getting a third hard, passionate working over and it was causing a major pressure to build up in my balls.

I saw the muscles in his pale arms tensed and bulging as he used his grip on the weight bar as leverage for the fuck. His stomach was rippling as he pounded his hot cock ball deep into my ass. My prone, helpless position also added to my natural teen horniness. All of this had an inevitable conclusion. I'd been so turned on by being tied up and relay fucked by three guys with a fourth waiting in the wings that it became too much pleasure to take.

I felt the cum reach critical mass in my balls as the warning tingle intensified. My slim, lean body locked solid, straining against its bonds as I arched my back. With what would have been a loud cry of ecstasy if it wasn't for the gag a bolt of cum raced down my cock and exploded out. I was so fucking horny and turned on that it arced through the air and splattered on my face. This was rapidly followed by a second jet which was also so powerful that it hit my face. Then 5 more jets of gradually diminishing reach and amount splattered on my sweaty heaving chest and stomach. I was gob smacked at the amount and intensity of my orgasm. I'd covered myself in my own cum which started to slowly cool. Wave after wave of intense pleasure flowed through me as I orgasmed, jet after jet squirting out of my cock.

As I orgasmed Ronald looked down at me with a knowing smile on his face, smug that he'd been the one to make me cum just from being fucked. From my point of view Arnold and Ethan had been just as instrumental and it just happened to be Ronald that was fucking me when I exploded. However, I'm sure Ronald attributed it to his big, thick cock and rough, hard, passionate fucking. That's not to detract from Ronald either. He really was a rough hard passionate fucker and his thick manhood always made my ass feel so good even though it stretched and penetrated it to the max. Having Ronald's swollen knob repeatedly hitting my prostate fuelled and prolonged my orgasm so much so that I almost fainted with pleasure.

My orgasm made my ass spasm uncontrollably around Ronald's thick thrusting cock and this caused him to start fucking me even faster and harder. This alone would be enough for my ass to feel the increased onslaught but my orgasm had made my ass even more sensitive and receptive to the rough hard fucking it was receiving. I was seeing stars of hard fucked pleasure, my ass throbbing and glowing. He was using all his strength to power his cock ball deep into my throbbing stretched ass, his groin loudly and rhythmically slapping against my buttocks. Each thrust of his cock into me sent waves of pleasure through the tender walls of my boy cunt.

I was being fucked like a whore and I was loving every second. If I knew bondage was so much fun I would have tried it earlier. I liked being helpless and unable to do anything except let these four men fuck me how they pleased and at present the third one was fucking me senseless. I guessed that Ronald was getting close to cumming. He'd been fucking me for ages but now he was fucking me even faster and harder than before, his fit, pale body glistening with sweat. Also, his breathing was becoming more laboured and his face scrunched in pleasure and exertion as the pressure increased in his balls.

My suspicions were confirmed a minute or so later when he groaned "Get ready prof, I'm going to breed your boy cunt." he rapidly pounded my ass, using all his strength to power the fuck. I started flexing my ass muscles on his pounding cock even faster and harder, gripping it as tight as I could to increase his pleasure and push him over the edge. It had the desired effect as a couple deeper thrusts of his cock and he buried it ball deep into my ass one last time. He arched his back and threw his head back as his groin slapped up hard against my buttocks. I saw his face contort in ecstasy as I felt his thick cock swell, throb, and pulse deep inside me. With a loud cry of pleasure his big erection started pumping jet after jet of hot cum deep into my ass. I muffled purrs of pleasure into my gag as I felt a third load of man cum being fired into my teen boy ass. I felt it bubble around his cock head as he thrust his cock with short stabs as he bucked and shuddered against me. I flexed my ass muscles on his penis to make him orgasm. I could tell that Ronald was having a big intense orgasm as it felt as if my ass had taken a cum enema. Almost as soon as Ronald finished cumming he pulled his cock from my ass which felt sore, full of cum and gapping open.

"You are such a hot fuck." He breathlessly gasped.

"Your go now Diageo." He added. After all this time I'd only just learnt the fourth guy's name. I only saw him a few times in class and he was about to plunder my sore, well fucked, used, cum filled ass. I watched as he walked over to me. I watched mesmerised as his big, thick Latino cock swung about as he walked towards me. It hung down under its own meaty weight and was a similar size to Ronald's, about 8.5 inches long but it was slightly thicker and uncut. My ass felt sore and tender and I knew that this feeling would soon intensify but my tool hungry nature overcame any apprehensions.

When he stood at the bottom of the bench, I could get a better look at him. He had a sexy round face with deep brown eyes and a Latino tan. I put him at about 22 or 23 and when he smiled his face lit up. I took in the sight of his olive tanned muscular arms and strong barrel chest. His stomach was flat and firm with a dusting of dark brown hairs leading in to a bush of dark brown pubes. I watched as with a lustful leer on his face he gripped his thick dusky cock and aimed it at my ass. I felt him press his swollen knob against my sore, puffy ass lips and felt the pressure increase. After already having taken three cocks, they gave little resistance and slid down over his flared cock head. I purred with pleasure into my gag as I felt his knob stretch and stimulate my ass lips. Even though they were tender the pleasure receptors in them were still running overtime. Diageo took the first thrust slowly and I could feel it all.

Once my sphincter passed the ridge of his knob they clamped around his thick meaty groin shaft. He then began to slowly force more of his big cock into me. His swollen knob forced open the throbbing, tender walls of my cum filled cunt, making the three loads of cum already up there squelch around his cock. Inch by inch he forced it in deep, his thick shaft stretching and stimulating my sphincter. His sexy Latino face had a look of ecstasy as he savoured the pleasure of slowly forcing his big cock into my cum filled ass. Soon he bottomed out with all 8.5 inches of his cock buried ball deep in my ass where he jerked and twitched it about as I flexed my ass muscles on it, gripping it tight causing him to gasp with pleasure and mutter something in what I thought was Spanish.

He then started pulling his package backwards and I felt my cum filled ass sucking and closing after his retreating cock, my swollen ass lips being pulled outwards. He pulled back until just his knob was inside my ass before he forced it back into me. It seemed that Diageo was going to take it nice and slow, wanting to savour the pleasure of fucking his professor. I would later find out that he was Brazilian and it was Portuguese that he was speaking. In Brazil shaggy haired blue-eyed boys were rare so I was as much a novelty to him as his Latino cock was to me and as such we took time to admire each other. I saw his tanned muscular arms tensed and bulging as he gripped the weights bar. His tanned lightly haired stomach rippled as he thrust his big thick cock ball deep in and out of my ass with long slow thrusts. I wished that my hands were free as I wanted to swarm them all over his body, feel the strength of his muscles under them and admire the colour contrast of my pale hands on his olive skin.

I was lost in admiring Diageo when Ronald, Ethan and Arnold came over. All three were hard, including Ronald who had only just cum a couple of minutes earlier into my ass. The three of them stood by my head with Arnold to my right, Ethan to my left and Ronald stood above me. They then began to wank their own cocks and I couldn't help but watch. My gaze switched from cock to cock and then back to Diageo. The sight of three hunky men tossing off over my face as a fourth fucked my ass was highly erotic.

I lost track of time as I was too caught on in watching what was going on. One moment I'd be watching Arnold's right hand rapidly sliding up and down his tanned, meaty manly cock and the next I'd be admiring Diageo's sexy Latino face and hunky body as he fucked me with his big thick manhood. My gaze would then switch to see Ronald's right hand wanking his pale, thick, meaty cock before switching to watch Ethan wanking his sexy, golden tanned cock. As this progressed Diageo started fucking me faster and harder, his big thick arousal stretching and filling my cum filled ass to the max. Never before had my ass felt so sore and used. It was throbbing and aching, my sphincter tender and swollen but it was definitely well worthwhile and I felt like such a slut, more so now that the new guy was fucking me.

Despite the way I maybe describing the feelings in my ass they were pleasurable rather than painful. All you bottom guys out there will know they pleasure you feel when your ass has received a serious fucking and mine had just received four in quick succession. I felt Diageo's swollen knob forcing open and caressing the throbbing sensitive walls of my ass, Arnold's, Ethan's, and Ronald's cum bubbling around his thrusting cock. His thick, meaty shaft was stretching my swollen ass lips to the max and stimulating them beyond belief. His groin was slapping up against my buttocks which were glowing from the repeated strikes taken in the course of four fucks. I felt like such a dirty, cock hungry slut and took pride in the fact that these four hunky men found me sexy enough to relay fuck me.

I don't know how long Diageo fucked me for but it felt like a pleasurably long time. It seemed with each thrust of his package he fucked me faster and harder so that by now he was hammering his impressive cock into me like a pile driver. Arnold, Ethan, and Ronald were also matching his increasing vigour by wanking their cocks faster. I was surrounded by four guys and I wondered which one would be the first to cum. I didn't have to wait long for an answer as a couple of minutes later Arnold pulled the gag from my mouth and aimed his cock at it. I opened my mouth just in time for Arnold to fire a jet of hot, thick, strong, tasty man spunk in it. It hit my tongue and immediately, its delicious taste made my taste buds jump with joy. That jet was rapidly followed by 4 more some of which went into my mouth and some splashed on my face. Arnold's face was scrunched up in ecstasy as he pumped his man spunk into my mouth, loudly moaning with pleasure. When he shot the last of his load into my mouth he smeared his rod in the cum on my face and then stuck it in my mouth. I began to greedily suck his salty man spunk off his cock which also had the lingering taste of my ass on it.

As I was sucking on Arnold's cock Ethan warned that he was close. Arnold pulled his cock from my mouth and I twisted my head to the left. I was just in time to take the first jet which squirted into my mouth. I'd already swallowed Arnold's cum but some had lingered on my tongue and now this was being added to by Ethan's cum which was slightly sweeter and less strong. I took Ethan's knob into my mouth and tightly clamped my lips around his shaft. I flicked the tip of my tongue on the sensitive underside of his knob as he blasted jet after jet of tasty cum into my mouth, coating my tongue with it as some trickled down my throat. I purred with pleasure as I savoured the cum in my mouth as Ethan gasped and groaned in the throes of orgasm.

"Oh, fuck yes." Diageo gasped in a thick accent as he banged his big thick cock in to my open hole at break neck speed. Obvious watching me greedily swallowing cum was a big turn on for him. He slammed his cock in and out of my ass a couple more times before he buried it in ball deep. His sexy face scrunched up and I felt his thick cock swell even more. I then felt it throb and pulse as it started blasting of hot cum deep inside my already cum filled ass. I muffled purrs of pleasure around Ethan's cock as the new guy came in my ass which was now so full of cum some of it started leaking out. Diageo fucked me with short stabs of his dick as he orgasmed and I flexed my ass muscles on his cock to fuel his orgasm and milk him dry. Seconds later Ronald gasped he was close and he quickly moved to my left, almost pushing Ethan out of the way before forcing his swollen, cut knob into my mouth. I began to greedily suck away on it, tasting my ass juice before that was replaced but the delicious taste of his hot thick man cum. Ronald was a naturally big spunker and even though he had recently cum in my ass he still shot a big healthy load of spunk into my mouth. As I was laid on my back I had to swallow it all down but my tongue received a good coating so I could savour the taste.

Diageo pulled his cock from my ass and I began to take stock of it and my hole felt like it was gapping open with sore, red puffy lips. My ass was so full of man spunk that it felt bloated and in desperate need to purge itself. The walls of my love chute were throbbing and tender and my prostate felt bruised. My buttocks were glowing from having four groins slapping against them and my body ached from being tied up for so long. My nostrils were full of the lingering smell of man sweat, hormones and gay sex. My mouth tingled with the taste of cum and ass juice and I was drained and exhausted. At the same time, I was elated at having received the best fucking of my young precious life and it would still be one of the best of my life. I felt so used and slutty and that was an enjoyable feeling. Arnold then untied me and passionately kissed me before breaking off and asking

"Did you like that, professor?"

"It was fucking ace." I breathlessly replied.

With that I went to the toilet as I could already feel cum dribbling down my legs. I purged my ass and had a shower. When I went downstairs, I noticed that I had over 10 missed calls from a number that I don't know, and some text messages. The messages started with a video, that was filmed of me having sex with the guys in the van. The person who sent the video was asking me to share the questions for the exam the next week, or he will post the video online and send it to the university causing me to be suspended.

I showed the messages to Arnold, who got very angry. Ronald and Ethan calmed him down, and said that we will find a way. Diageo was the class representative and had every student phone number, so they asked him to look up the number and he found out it was Matt, one of the class mates.

"Don't worry about it" Arnold said to me. "We will sort it out"

"Let's go guys, I know where he lives" Diageo said.

An hour later, the guys came back with Matt's camera and phone. They assured me that they taught Matt a lesson and that there is nothing he can do about this. They made sure the video is completely deleted. "Thank you, guys, so much" I said. Arnold came to me and said "I love you, and I will let nothing bad happen to you" We kissed passionately then he carried me to bed and we fell asleep in each other arms.